Praise for *I'm With Cupid*

"Readers are in for a wild and hilarious ride from upcoming installments in the Switched at First Kiss series."

—Booklist

"A cute and mild love story with a dash of supernatural charm that dives a little deeper with its exploration of death and love."

—School Library Journal

"As always, Staniszewski provides a deft mix of comedy and sensitive, deeper themes, making her book not only entertaining, but one that offers wisdom. She knows where to mine the humor from middle school life but does not sacrifice her characterizations for easy laughs. Light—but not lightweight—fun for preteens."

—Kirkus Reviews

Praise for *The Dirt Diary*

"Holy fried onion rings! Fun from beginning to end."

—Wendy Mass, *New York Times* bestselling author of
11 Birthdays and *The Candymakers*

"I LOVED it…sweet, sensitive, and delicious!"

—Erin Dionne, author of
Models Don't Eat Chocolate Cookies

"Confidently addressing a number of common tween troubles that include bullying, parental divorce, and peer pressure, Staniszewski introduces a determined eighth grader desperate to get her separated parents back together in this humorous problem novel."

—*Publishers Weekly*

"Staniszewski neatly captures the pain of a shy young girl with newly separated parents… The quick pace and creative story line will attract those in the mood for an undemanding, light read."

—*Kirkus Reviews*

Praise for *The Prank List*

"*The Prank List* hooks readers with snappy dialogue from the beginning... Rachel is a likable character for middle school readers, who will relate to her problems."

—*VOYA*

"Staniszewski keeps the focus on comedy...but she lets her story become a bit more serious with the pranks Rachel plays. Clearly, Rachel will learn a few life lessons as she stumbles through her summer, but they go down easy in this narrative peppered with such amusing catchphrases as 'Oh my goldfish' and 'What the Shrek?' Gentle fun laced with equally gentle wisdom."

—*Kirkus Reviews*

"Tween readers who find Rachel endearing will find a fast-paced comedy of errors."

—*School Library Journal*

Praise for
My Very UnFairy Tale Life

"Anna Staniszewski creates a magical world that's totally relatable. You'll find yourself wishing you were alongside Jenny fighting against unicorns (who aren't as peaceful as you think) and traveling to fantastical realms."

—GirlsLife.com

"A light comic romp… An eye for imaginative detail mixes with these likable characters and a theme of empathy for others to keep the story appropriate to a younger audience, who easily will identify with Jenny. Charming."

—*Kirkus Reviews*

"Staniszewski's debut is a speedy and amusing ride that displays a confident, on-the-mark brand of humor, mostly through Jenny's wisecracking narration…will keep readers entertained."

—*Publishers Weekly*

Match Me If You Can

SWITCHED AT
FIRST
KISS

Also by Anna Staniszewski

My Very UnFairy Tale Life Series

My Very UnFairy Tale Life

My Epic Fairy Tale Fail

My Sort of Fairy Tale Ending

The Dirt Diary Series

The Dirt Diary

The Prank List

The Gossip File

The Truth Game

Switched at First Kiss Series

I'm With Cupid

Finders Reapers

Match Me If You Can

SWITCHED AT
FIRST
KISS

ANNA **STANISZEWSKI**

sourcebooks
jabberwocky

Published by Sourcebooks Jabberwocky, an imprint of Sourcebooks, Inc.
P.O. Box 4410, Naperville, Illinois 60567-4410
(630) 961-3900
Fax: (630) 961-2168
www.sourcebooks.com

Library of Congress Cataloging-in-Publication data is on file with the publisher.

Source of Production: Versa Press, East Peoria, Illinois, USA
Date of Production: November 2016
Run Number: 5007998

Printed and bound in the United States of America.
VP 10 9 8 7 6 5 4 3 2 1

For Ray. Collect all three!

Chapter 1

Lena hated surprises. And yet here she was in her mom's car, winding through Phoenix during morning rush hour, on the way to some mysterious location.

"We're not going to your hospital, are we?" Lena asked. Normally, she didn't mind hospitals, and she was curious about her mom's job as a nurse, but Lena wanted to stay far away from illness and death while she was visiting her mom over winter break. Then she'd really feel as if she were on vacation.

Her mom only smiled and said, "Wait and see."

Lena groaned. "Mom! Don't you remember what happened when you tried to throw me a surprise party at the zoo when I was little? I still can't go past that place without feeling sick to my stomach."

"Of course I remember. Just because I haven't been around for a while doesn't mean…" Her mom cleared her throat. "You'll like this surprise. I promise."

"Does it have anything to do with your assignments?" Lena

asked, perking up. She had recently found out that she and her mom shared a huge supernatural secret: they were both soul collectors, people who helped guide souls into the After. Except, after years of collecting souls, Lena's mom had recently been promoted to the role of soul hunter, which meant she tracked down the souls that got away. Lena couldn't wait to hear more about the other parts of her mom's job, especially since it sounded a lot more exciting than hers.

"No, it's nothing otherworldly." Her mom honked her horn. "I just hope we get there on time!"

"On time for what?" Lena asked, but all she got in return was another mysterious smile.

As they pulled to a stoplight, Lena suddenly sank back in her seat as a wave of dizziness swept over her. A second later, a strange ringing echoed in her ears. What was going on? She'd felt a little light-headed on the plane ride yesterday, but it had been nothing like this.

All at once, the spinning and ear-ringing stopped, and she was fine again. Huh. Probably jet lag. Since Lena had never even traveled out of the state before, let alone a couple of time zones over, it made sense that her body would be a little confused.

"Are you okay?" her mom asked. "You look pale."

"Just tired," Lena said. Then she laughed softly. "We probably shouldn't have stayed up so late last night talking about quilting patterns!"

Lena's phone beeped in her pocket. It was a message from her boyfriend Marcus: What do you think about a light-up bow tie for the NYE dance? Also, I miss you.

She couldn't help grinning. Marcus had been talking about the New Year's Eve dance at the Y for days. He was convinced that if they kissed at midnight, next year would be just about perfect. Not only was Marcus a total romantic, but he was also a supernatural matchmaker—like Cupid but without the diaper—which meant he spent way too much time thinking about mushy stuff. Lena didn't believe in superstitions, but she was excited to be able to check "first dance" off her list of things to accomplish before she turned fourteen. As far as she was concerned, things between her and Marcus were already pretty perfect.

I miss you too, she wrote back. But NO glowing accessories. With our luck, you'll get electrocuted!

Finally, her mom stopped the car in front of an old theater. "Ta-dah!" she said. "It's your Christmas present!"

"Are we going to see a show?" Lena asked, her nerves melting away.

"Better than that. *You're* going to be *in* a show!"

Lena stared at her. "Huh?"

"My coworker's cousin runs a theater workshop for young people during winter break," she said, "and I was able to get you in at the last minute. At the end of the week, they put on a short production, and everyone in the workshop gets a part. Isn't that great?"

Lena blinked. "Really? You mean I'll finally get to be in an actual play?" She'd been dreaming about being onstage for years, but so far, all her attempts had failed. Maybe this would finally be her chance. She could picture it already, standing in front of a big crowd in a fancy costume, making people laugh and maybe even cry. "Mom, thank you! This is amazing!"

She threw her arms around her mom and gave her an awkward hug over the gearshift. After three years of them being apart, it still felt strange to have her mom around to hug whenever Lena felt like it, but she was starting to get used to it.

"You're welcome," her mom said as Lena finally let her go. "Now let's head inside. We don't want to be late."

"Wait, you're coming in with me?"

"Of course! It's like the first day of school, right? I want to make sure to see you off."

Lena swallowed as she spotted a couple of other kids her age going into the theater alone. Yes, this was like the first day of school. You didn't want your parents walking in with you then either.

"Um, thanks. That's really nice, but I'll be okay by myself."

"Are you sure? You won't know anyone, and you might not know where you're going and—"

"Mom, I'll be fine!" Lena said with a laugh. "I've been doing stuff on my own for years."

Her mom held up her hands in defeat. "You're right. Have fun. I'll pick you up at one, okay?" Then she handed Lena a lunchbox she'd packed for the occasion and finally let her go.

Lena practically tumbled out of the car, her body humming with excitement. She quickly sent Marcus a message telling him about the class. She could imagine him in his room, working on one of his model spaceships, restoring it so it was almost as good as new. After the crazy few months they'd had—swapping powers and then swapping them back only to have them go totally overboard—Marcus had definitely earned some quiet time. They both had.

When Lena glanced up from her phone, she expected her mom's car to be gone, but her mom was still sitting at the curb, obviously waiting for Lena to go inside. Lena gave her one last wave and then headed into the theater.

The first thing Lena smelled as she went into the lobby was buttered popcorn. She paused. In her experience, that scent meant a wandering spirit was nearby. But then she spotted the concession stand, cranking out popcorn for the matinee, and she had to laugh at herself. She'd gotten so used to worrying about souls running around that it was hard to relax. But all the drama from the past couple of months was over. Now that things between Lena and Marcus were great—and the two of them were determined to keep them that way—there was no need to worry.

That's awesome! Marcus wrote back. Break lots of legs!

Lena chuckled and then poked her head into the theater. She sucked in a breath at the sight of the gilded ceilings, red velvet curtains, and colorful murals on the walls. The place could probably use a good cleaning and a fresh coat of paint, but it was still amazing. Lena couldn't believe that *she* was going to perform here!

As the door closed behind her, Lena spotted a circle of about ten kids her age sitting on the stage. Inside the circle, a tall woman was standing very still and speaking in a slow, steady voice about the importance of being punctual.

Suddenly, the woman glanced up at her and paused. "Lena Perris?" she asked.

"I-I'm sorry I'm late," Lena said, rushing forward, though it was only one minute past nine. Even by her dad's standards, that meant she was on time.

"I'm Miss Fine," the woman said. "Join us." She held out

a preprinted name tag. Lena grabbed it and attached it to her shirt before finding a spot in the circle. Then she tried to focus on what Miss Fine was saying about the expectations for the week. There were a lot of them. Being on time. Respecting your fellow actors. Knowing all of your lines.

As she talked, some of the other kids started to look nervous, but Lena had to smother a smile. This was so much better than her school's production of *Alice in Wonderland*. That show had gone okay in the end—despite Lena accidentally crash-landing onstage during it—but Lena couldn't help thinking it would have gone even better if the director had been a lot stricter. Maybe then the Cheshire Cat wouldn't have totally blanked on his lines halfway through opening night.

"Any questions?" Miss Fine asked when she was done.

"What show are we doing?" a boy with wild blond curls asked. His name tag said his name was Zade, which Lena thought made him sound like someone from a boy band. He even had the hair to match.

"During the showcase, we'll be performing selected scenes from *Peter Pan*," Miss Fine answered. A rumble of excitement passed through the group.

"Is that a real trapdoor in the stage?" a boy named Luis asked, pointing to the center of the stage. "Will we get to fall through it?"

Miss Fine smiled. "It *is* a working trapdoor, but I don't think any of our scenes will require it." She clapped her hands. "Okay. If there are no more questions—"

"Is it true this theater is haunted?" a girl named Shontelle broke in.

Lena tensed for a second, but Miss Fine chuckled and said, "You sound like my grandmother. All old theaters have stories about them. I've done several workshops and plays here, and I really don't think we have anything to worry about."

"But I heard they had to cancel a couple of shows last year because weird stuff kept happening," Shontelle said. "Doors slamming and people getting locked in closets and—"

"It's true one show had to be called off, but it was because the cast got the flu," Miss Fine interrupted. "The other production was only postponed due to some electrical problems."

Lena glanced around, trying to find any hint of the hazy sparks that meant a wandering soul was nearby. But the theater was dark except for the overhead stage lights.

"Are you sure?" Shontelle clearly didn't want to let it drop. "Because I heard—" Suddenly, she jumped. "Ouch!" she cried, gripping her arm. "Something just pinched me!"

"Probably a bug," Luis said from across the circle. "There was a scorpion in my kitchen this morning. It was so cool."

That didn't seem to make Shontelle feel any better.

"Or maybe a bird pooped on you," Zade chimed in. When everyone gave him puzzled looks, he pointed up. "There are birds living above the stage. I heard them flapping around."

Lena glanced up and, sure enough, spotted a pigeon roosting above one of the curtains.

"Okay, okay," Miss Fine said. "We're getting off track. Yes, there are birds in the theater, but the management has promised me they'll be gone before our show. And as far as I know, there are no scorpions and no ghosts. Okay?" She looked at Shontelle, who was still rubbing her arm above the elbow. The girl gave a weak shrug.

Miss Fine seemed happy with that response, because she clapped her hands again and added, "Now, let's get up and do some physical warm-ups. We have plenty of work ahead if we want to be ready for our show on New Year's Eve."

Lena blinked. "Wait. New Year's Eve?"

"That's right," Miss Fine said. "Our performance will be a matinee on December 31. Is that a problem?"

"I-I'm supposed to fly home that morning."

Miss Fine waved her hand dismissively. "It's already taken care of. When I spoke to your mother about signing you up for this class, she changed your plane ticket to the following day. Didn't she tell you?"

"Oh." No, her mom hadn't told her.

Miss Fine glanced back at the other kids. "Now, everyone find a spot on the stage, and let's do some jumping jacks!"

As Lena started to go through the boot camp regimen Miss Fine had in store for them, her mind swirled. How would she tell Marcus that she couldn't make it to the New Year's Eve dance? He'd be crushed! And why hadn't her mom checked with her before changing Lena's plane ticket?

Then again, Marcus knew how important being onstage was to her. If they did their midnight kiss a little late, maybe it would be okay. How much difference could a few hours really make? Still, she dreaded having to break the news to Marcus.

"Lena, get your head in the game!" Miss Fine hollered like a drill sergeant. "Do those squats like you mean them!"

Lena's muscles ached, and her lungs heaved for breath, but she couldn't help smiling. Finally, here was a director as serious about theater as she was. This was going to be one amazing vacation.

Chapter 2

So far, this was turning out to be a terrible vacation. Marcus had wanted to lock himself in his room and work on his models for most of winter break, but instead, over Christmas breakfast, his dad had declared that he was remodeling the bathroom and that Marcus and his sister, Ann-Marie, would be helping. Marcus was a total weakling compared to his athlete sister, a fact that had become painfully obvious when she'd lifted two packs of bathroom tiles while Marcus had struggled to carry just one. That pretty much set the tone for the whole project.

Now on day two of being crammed into the bathroom with his dad and sister, Marcus was covered in grout and dust and sweat, doing his best to hold a pipe steady while his dad kept yelling at him to hold still. Marcus was so busy trying not to move—or even breathe—that he got light-headed for a minute and had to sit down and wait for the ringing in his ears to fade. Meanwhile, his sister was pulling up tile as if she'd been doing it from birth. Show-off.

As Marcus finally got back to work, his mom poked her head into the bathroom. "Do you really have to do this now? I can't concentrate with all the noise." She looked exhausted, and there were chunks of dough in her hair. Normally, Marcus's mom made sculptures out of trash, but this time, she'd decided to use raw pizza dough. That meant the fridge was crammed full of dough balls, and the whole house smelled like moldy bread. And since her new show was opening in a couple of weeks, she'd been even more frazzled than normal, especially since the sculptures kept sagging.

"How much concentration do dough blobs take?" Marcus's dad said with a chuckle, brushing some dust off his forehead.

Marcus's mom pursed her lips. "Just because you don't understand my art doesn't mean you can make fun of it."

Uh-oh. Marcus and Ann-Marie exchanged looks. The air in the tiny bathroom was suddenly charged with tension. No doubt, their parents were about to have another one of their fights. His parents' relationship had always had rough patches, but these days, his mom and dad seemed to argue about everything, even about who should turn off the porch light at night. The fights were bad enough when Marcus had to listen to them through his bedroom wall. He definitely couldn't handle being in the middle of one in a tiny bathroom.

At that moment, a miracle happened. Marcus's phone

buzzed. It was a message from his boss Eduardo, a.k.a. Eddie. New love match in an hour. Then it gave the location and target.

"I have to go," Marcus said, letting go of the pipe. "Um, I forgot I have to swing by the library."

"What, *now*?" his dad boomed.

"It's for a, um, geography project." Marcus hated lying to his parents—and he wasn't all that good at it—but he figured a homework-related excuse would get him off the hook. It always worked for Ann-Marie.

"Fine," his dad said, "but I expect you to get an A on this assignment or else."

"Yes, sir."

"I should get back to work," his mom said as Marcus squeezed past her and out into the hallway. Then she sighed deeply and went back to her basement studio. Phew. Another blowout parent fight averted.

Marcus hurried to change out of his dirty clothes. As he pulled on a clean sweater, his phone beeped again. But this time, it was a message from Lena. His heart trilled with excitement for a second until he actually read what she'd written.

So sorry but I can't make it to the NYE dance. My theater class has its show that day.

Marcus couldn't believe it. But what about our kiss at midnight? he wrote back. We can't tempt fate. It already likes messing with us!

He slowly laced up his sneakers, desperately hoping she'd write back and tell him he was right. He knew Lena thought he was a hopeless romantic. She poked fun at him every time he left her a mushy note or insisted on celebrating yet another special occasion. But she couldn't ignore something this big, could she?

Will make it up to you, she finally wrote back. I promise!!

He sighed in disappointment. How was he supposed to welcome the new year without his girlfriend at his side? But, he reminded himself, Lena finally had a chance to be in a real show. This was her dream. Even though he was bummed for himself, he had to be happy for her.

Okay, he wrote. We'll do something superspecial when you get back. Maybe he *was* taking this tradition thing a little too seriously. He just didn't want to risk anything else going wrong between him and Lena.

Marcus's sister was waiting for him in the hallway when he opened his bedroom door. "Since when do you take geography?" she asked, her arms crossed in front of her chest. "Come on. Where are you really going?"

"None of your business," he said, pushing past her. Then he paused. "Don't tell Dad, okay?"

"Fine, but you have to do me a favor." For some reason, Ann-Marie's cheeks turned a little pink. Marcus had hardly ever seen his sister blush before. "I have a...a date later, but I don't want Dad to know about it. You know how he is about stuff that takes away from track and homework."

"A date?" Marcus repeated, his conversation with Lena momentarily forgotten. "With Peter Chung?"

"Sh!" Ann-Marie hissed, glancing down the empty hallway. "Do you want Dad to hear you? It's not a big deal. We're just going to get some burgers."

"I thought you didn't eat red meat," Marcus couldn't help saying. His sister was always sipping gross vegetarian "power smoothies" and pointing out the empty calories in everything Marcus put on his plate.

"I can make an exception once in a while, can't I? Anyway, can I tell Dad that you called from the library and begged me to come help you with your project?"

"You think he'll actually believe that?"

Ann-Marie shrugged. "He will if I say it. So, can you help me?" She paused a second and then, to Marcus's shock, added, "Please?"

It was weird to have his sister begging for his help. Usually, it was the other way around. But Marcus knew he had to say yes. His sister's aura had been different lately—not quite gray but not quite yellow—which meant she might be on the verge of a love boost. He was a matchmaker, after all. He had to help people get together, whether they were officially his assignments or not.

"Fine," he said. "But not a word about geography to Dad, okay?"

Marcus's phone beeped, reminding him he only had thirty minutes to get to his matching location. He didn't have time to worry about his sister's relationships. He had work to do.

Chapter 3

When Marcus got to the mall, he wove his way through the after-Christmas-sale crowds until he got to the comic book store. Inside, he scanned the handful of shoppers, trying to spot "Albert Landry, age fifteen." For some reason, the name sounded familiar—maybe he was in Ann-Marie's grade?—but Marcus didn't see anyone he recognized, and there was no telltale aura telling him that someone was ready for a love boost.

He still had ten minutes before the match, so he plopped down on a bench outside the store and tried to casually study the crowd around him, looking for gray auras.

"Marcus Torelli?" someone said behind him.

He turned to find Connie Reynolds, one of the most popular girls in the eighth grade and the school's biggest gossip, coming toward him. For some reason, she seemed excited to see him.

"How's your vacation going so far?" She frowned. "Is that dirt in your hair?"

He quickly brushed at his thick mop, sending grout dust into the air. Gross. "Vacation is fine. Um, grimy, I guess. What are you doing here?" He realized how stupid the question was after he'd asked it. Didn't girls like Connie pretty much live at the mall?

"I'm meeting my cousin. She's finally going to let me give her a makeover." She rolled her eyes and adjusted her scarf, a hideous purple thing with white horses all over it. "She has *no* fashion sense." Connie's face brightened. "You and Lena are coming to the New Year's Eve dance at the Y, right? My mom and I are in charge of decorations. It's going to be so much fun!"

"Oh, um…" Marcus swallowed. "It turns out Lena won't be home from Arizona in time."

Connie's lip-glossed mouth sagged open. "But isn't it totally bad luck if you don't do a midnight kiss with the person you want to be with the next year?"

"It's not a big deal," he mumbled, not meeting her eyes.

"Well, next time you talk to her, you tell her that I won't take no for an answer!" Connie said.

Marcus chuckled. "I'll tell her tonight. We have a phone call scheduled after dinner."

Connie raised an eyebrow. "Scheduled? How romantic."

"I know, but Lena's pretty busy." It had been Lena's idea

to do the scheduled calls. Marcus didn't love how restricting they were, but it was better than not being able to talk to each other at all.

Connie nodded. "Well, if you don't want to sit around waiting for her to call, a bunch of us are going to a trampoline park tomorrow afternoon. You should come!" She started listing off people who were going to be there, and Marcus realized he'd met a couple of them while doing sets for the school play. Still, he wasn't the kind of person who went to that kind of thing, not without Lena at his side to keep him from totally embarrassing himself.

"Thanks, but I'm pretty busy helping my dad do stuff around the house." A soft alarm sounded on his phone, reminding him that it was almost time for his match. "I have to go," Marcus said, getting to his feet. "See you around, okay?"

"At the New Year's Eve dance!" Connie cooed. "Promise me you'll be there, even if Lena's not back yet!"

"Um, yeah, okay," he said, figuring it was quicker not to fight her. If he simply didn't show up at the dance on Thursday, he doubted Connie would even notice.

Then, to Marcus's horror, she pulled him in for a hug. "It was so great to see you!" she said as if they hadn't sat next to each other in English the other day. Then she released him and dashed away.

His face hot, Marcus went back into the comic book store and spotted a familiar-looking skinny guy by the superhero comics. It took Marcus a minute to place him, but then he remembered: he'd seen the guy at a high school academic award ceremony that Marcus's parents had dragged him to. This was the guy who'd beaten Ann-Marie out for top GPA last year. Now that Marcus thought about it, he remembered that her archrival's name had been Albert. And now Marcus was supposed to fix him up with someone.

When Marcus squinted, sure enough, he spotted a gray aura over Albert's head. Marcus's phone started beeping again, telling him he only had two minutes before the match.

After taking a deep breath to steady himself, he called up his energy. Normally, his fingers flared to life with a deep red flame. But this time, nothing happened.

Marcus stared at his fingers. He'd had trouble with his powers in the past—they'd glowed the wrong color and flickered in and out before—but they'd never simply not worked like this. Meanwhile, Albert Landry was shuffling toward the exit.

No!

Marcus had to zap him. Otherwise, the whole balance of the universe could be knocked out of whack!

He desperately tried to call up his energy again, but his hands were as nonglowing as ever. What was going on?

Marcus's phone was beeping and beeping, but all he could do was stand there frozen. Then Albert went through the door, and Marcus darted after him. He had no idea who Albert was supposed to be matched with. Someone in the comic shop? There weren't any other people their age here, so maybe not. Maybe that meant Marcus still had a chance.

No matter what, he couldn't let Albert get away.

Marcus left the store and frantically searched the crowd. He finally spotted Albert stooped over a water fountain, his unkempt hair nearly covering his face.

"Hey, Albert, wait up!" Marcus found himself calling out.

Albert turned toward him, wiping water from his chin. Then he started to walk away, as if he was certain no one could be talking to him.

Desperate, Marcus sprinted over and grabbed his arm. "Hey, hold on a sec."

Albert flinched away from his touch. "What—what do you want?" he asked, his voice low and creaky, as if it wasn't used very often.

"I just…" Marcus scrambled to come up with an excuse. "You're the one who beat my sister out for top GPA last year, right? Ann-Marie Torelli?"

Albert's eyebrows arched in surprise. "She's your sister?"

"Yup."

"Oh." Albert looked at his feet. "She's beating me this year. I just found out the other day. She's a whole point ahead."

"Sorry," Marcus said, scanning the people walking by. Did any of them look like someone Albert was supposed to be matched with? Not unless the poor guy was meant to wind up with an old lady.

"I have to go," Albert said, inching away.

"Wait!" He had to at least figure out who Albert was supposed to end up with. Then maybe he could find a way to fix the situation without the cosmic balance totally getting messed up. "Um, do you have a crush on anyone?"

Albert stepped back as if he'd been slapped. "Wh-what?" Then his eyes narrowed in suspicion. "Who told you? Was it the parrot at the pet store?" He motioned toward the other end of the mall. "I knew he'd repeat what I said!"

Marcus couldn't believe how crazy that sounded, but he nodded and said, "Yeah, I've, um, been listening to parrot gossip. So it's true? You really like her?"

Albert blinked.

"Or him?" Marcus tried again.

But Albert wasn't paying attention. He was looking past Marcus at someone inside the Burger Shack. When Marcus turned, he almost laughed when he spotted his sister sitting at a window booth with Peter Chung, sipping milk shakes and looking like the perfect couple. Of course he'd bump into his sister here of all places.

Except something was off. Ann-Marie was with the guy she supposedly liked, and yet she kept checking her phone as if she couldn't wait to get out of there. Not exactly how Marcus expected her to act when she was with her love match.

Albert let out a weird choking sound beside him, and Marcus noticed a stricken look on Albert's face as he watched the couple too. Things suddenly clicked.

"Wait, you have a crush on *my sister*?" Marcus asked. But the answer was obvious. You didn't need to be a matchmaker to know that Albert was hopelessly in love with Ann-Marie. And based on the look of pure hatred that she flashed back at Albert the minute she saw him, you didn't need to be a matchmaker to know that Ann-Marie absolutely, one hundred percent did not feel the same way.

Chapter 4

O kay, now we're going to get in pairs and work on training our bodies to take on the physicality of other people,"
Miss Fine said to the class after a snack break. Normally,
Lena would have been embarrassed to nibble on the little-kid
food her mom had packed for her—orange slices and animal
crackers—while everyone else crunched on bags of chips, but
she'd been too busy feeling bad about not being able to make
it to the New Year's Eve dance.

She'd make it up to Marcus when she got back home. Somehow.

"Lena?" Miss Fine asked. "Do you need a partner?"

Lena jumped. "W-what?" She realized the only person who
wasn't already paired with someone was Zade. He did not look
happy when she went over to him.

"Is the whole class going to be like this?" he asked as they
went to the corner of the stage.

"Like what?" So far, Lena thought the class was going great.

"So strict? I mean, when is it going to be fun? I only signed up for this because I thought we'd play games and stuff. That's what we do in the drama club at school."

"Trust me, this is so much better than playing games," Lena said. "We're actually learning how to be better actors."

"The whole point of vacation is to not have to learn stuff." He sighed. "Okay, do you want me to walk first and you copy me or the other way around?"

"I'll move around first," Lena said.

She started strolling across the stage, suddenly very conscious of her body's every movement. When she glanced behind her, she saw Zade moving stiffly and briskly, like a windup toy. He was intently chewing on his bottom lip as if he were deep in thought.

"That's not how I look!" she said.

He laughed and started exaggerating each step even more. "Hello, I am Lena," he said in a robotic voice. "I do not bend my knees when I walk."

"Stop it!" Lena cried, but she couldn't help laughing. She had to admit that she *was* kind of stiff. Marcus had once poked fun at her for walking as if she had a surfboard glued to her spine.

"Zade! Lena!" Miss Fine called across the stage. "I want to see you two taking this exercise seriously!"

Lena's smile vanished, and her cheeks grew hot. "Let's switch," she said.

Zade shrugged and then started walking around the stage like himself, shuffling his left foot a bit with each step. Lena studied him for a second and then began following him around, trying to mimic his uneven gait.

"That's a good start, Lena," Miss Fine said, coming over. "But try to focus on the smaller details. Look how loose Zade's limbs are, how relaxed."

Lena squinted in concentration, focusing on Zade's every movement. Then she made her muscles go slack, so that her arms and legs were flopping around by her sides and her legs were pieces of spaghetti beneath her.

"Good!" Miss Fine said. "Now you're really getting it."

Even though Lena's head hurt from concentrating so hard, she couldn't help beaming as Miss Fine moved on to the next pair.

At the end of class, Miss Fine told everyone to start learning their lines and then went around from person to person giving them individual assignments for the next day. Lena held her breath as Miss Fine went up to Zade, knowing that her homework would be next.

"Zade," Miss Fine said, "I appreciate your sense of humor, but you need to know when to turn it off. Acting is work. You need to treat it that way."

Zade didn't look happy, but he nodded. Lena felt a tiny bit bad for him, but he'd be glad at the end of the week when his acting skills were even better.

"And finally, Lena," Miss Fine said. "I can see you take acting very seriously. As you can tell, I do too. I have a feeling you're going to be my star pupil." She started to walk away.

"Wait," Lena said. "What's my homework?"

Miss Fine smiled. "Just keep up the good work," she said.

Lena thought she might burst from happiness. She was floating on a cloud even when Miss Fine announced that they would be doing scenes from *Peter Pan* with the kids they'd been partnered with for the movement exercise. Although that meant Lena was stuck with "I just wanna have fun" Zade for the rest of the week, it didn't matter. Lena would make it work somehow.

As the kids headed home, actors from the matinee started to come into the theater. Lena took her time packing up her things so she could observe the professional actors humming to themselves and doing vocal exercises, getting ready to be in a real show. When she tiptoed out of the theater, Lena couldn't help imagining being in their shoes one day.

She headed through the lobby and was about to go outside to find her mom when a creepy feeling swept over her. As if someone were standing directly behind her. But when Lena spun around, all she saw was the antique piano in the corner of the lobby. A moment later, Miss Fine emerged through the theater doors.

"Still here?" Miss Fine asked. Then she smiled. "I know you're a dedicated actress, but you can't live here!" Suddenly, a door slammed somewhere, and Miss Fine jumped, her smile fading. She glanced over her shoulder and said, "I'll see you tomorrow, okay?"

As Lena watched her disappear through a door marked "Employees Only," she noticed something—a clump of light trailing after Miss Fine. It was a soul! Miss Fine was wrong. There *was* a ghost in the theater.

"Hey!" Lena called, rushing after the ball of light as it disappeared through the door. "Wait!"

But when Lena tried to pull the door open, it was locked. And any trace of the soul had disappeared.

"Tell me all about the class," Lena's mom said over sandwiches at a little deli near the theater. "Did you like the other kids? Was the teacher nice?"

Lena had to laugh. "Mom, you're acting like it was my first day of kindergarten! But yeah, everyone was okay. I'm not sure my scene partner actually wants to be there though."

"Should I talk to the teacher about having you switch partners?"

"What? No! It's fine. I'll figure it out."

Her mom shrugged as she worked on sawing her tuna sandwich in half with a flimsy plastic knife. "I just want this class to be a good experience, that's all."

"I know. And it's amazing. Except..." Lena considered telling her mom about the soul she'd seen floating after Miss Fine. After all, her mom was a soul hunter now. This was her territory.

"Except what?" her mom asked.

No, Lena decided. This was supposed to be their mother/daughter bonding week. Surely there was another soul hunter who could take care of it. "Nothing. It's great. But why didn't you ask me before changing my plane ticket?"

Her mom shrugged. "I didn't think it would matter. You don't start school again until Monday."

"I promised Marcus I'd be home for the New Year's Eve dance. He really wants us to be together at midnight."

"Midnight?" Her mom eye's widened. "Your father was going to let you stay out by yourself until midnight? How would you get home?"

"It's a special occasion," Lena said. "And I wouldn't be by myself. All my friends will be there. I was going to get a ride home with Abigail."

Her mom shook her head. "I'm still not sure I like the sound of that, but you get to be in a play instead. Doesn't that make up for it?"

"It does," Lena said. "The class is the perfect present. I just wish you'd asked me about changing my flight before you did it."

"I understand," her mom said. "Next time, I'll check with you first." Her face brightened. "So what do you want to do after we eat? My friend has a daughter around your age. If you want, I can see if I can set up a playdate."

Lena started to laugh until she saw that her mom was serious. "Um, that's okay. I had some stuff I thought you and I could do together." Now that she and her mom had been reunited, she wanted to make sure they didn't miss their chance to reconnect. "There's a quilt exhibit at a museum near here, or maybe we could go check out some fabric stores. I noticed your apartment is really bare. The quilt I made you for Christmas would look good in the living room, but maybe we can make another one to hang in the guest room."

"I haven't had much time for quilting recently, or for anything else for that matter. I thought of trying out for a play when I first moved here, but I haven't had time." She laughed. "And if I'm being honest, I'm a little nervous about the idea. I haven't been onstage in years!" She reached over and started cutting up Lena's sandwich too.

"Mom? What are you doing?"

"These sandwiches are so big. I figured it would be easier for you to eat it this way."

Before Lena could remind her mom that she was thirteen now and didn't need someone to cut food up for her, her phone started beeping. A second later, so did her mom's.

There was a message from Eddie waiting on Lena's phone, and it seemed like one he was sending out to all of his employees.

Be advised that we are experiencing some power disruptions at this time. If you are on assignment, continue to the best of your ability. If you need help, contact me, and I'll get back to you as soon as I can.

"That's weird," Lena said to her mom. "Eddie just contacted me and said there are—"

"Power disruptions?" her mom asked. "I got the same message from my boss Yvonne."

Lena grabbed her mom's phone and compared the two messages. They were identical. "What does it mean?"

Her mom shook her head, a deep wrinkle appearing between her eyebrows. "I don't know, but I've never gotten a message like this. And I've been a soul collector since before you were born."

Lena's phone beeped again, and she expected it to be another message from Eddie. But it was from Marcus. My powers are out! Eddie says it's an outage. Are you okay?

Lena swallowed. I'm fine, she wrote back. But she didn't feel fine. She'd been hoping things were finally back to normal with their powers, with her family, with everything. But if people all over the country had lost their powers, that meant something had to be really wrong.

Chapter 5

Marcus hovered near his front door, waiting for the doorbell to ring. He normally hated for people to come over and see his disaster of a house, filled with Ann-Marie's gym stuff and reeking of his mom's latest art project, but Natalie had insisted on coming to him.

He'd been hoping to talk to Eddie instead, but Marcus's supernatural boss had sent his daughter in his place. Marcus wasn't sure he completely trusted Natalie after she'd lied about being a soul collector and a bunch of other stuff, but she was also a seer. Being able to peek into the future had to be helpful in situations like this, right?

As he waited, Marcus paced back and forth in the hallway until his dad yelled at him to stop wearing out the carpet. Then he sat on the couch and practically strangled a pillow with his restless fingers.

Ever since he and Lena had kissed at Connie Reynolds's party a few months ago and swapped powers, the supernatural world had been upside down. Just when they thought things were fixed, they'd go crazy again. How could they be sure this mess wasn't somehow their fault too?

When the doorbell finally rang, Marcus jumped up and opened it before anyone else could get it. Then he hurried outside and closed the door behind him, so that he and Natalie could talk on the porch.

"Um, hi," she said, pulling her coat tighter around her. "Is everything okay?" Clearly, she'd been expecting him to ask her in.

"You tell me," Marcus said. "I can't get ahold of your dad."

"He's been on the phone all day, trying to figure stuff out. This outage thing is pretty serious. That's why he sent me to talk to you instead of coming himself."

"So the outage is happening everywhere?"

Natalie sighed. "At first we thought it was only in the United States, but now it looks like it's in other countries too."

"But people can't *not* die or *not* fall in love! That will mess everything up!"

"My dad's working on it with the boss lady," Natalie said. "They're hoping people can do their assignments without their powers. Can you still see auras?"

He nodded. "I checked my sister's after I got the message, and it's still kind of yellow, like she might get a love boost soon.

The guy she's been hanging out with is so perfect for her. I figured it would have already happened." Marcus sighed. Maybe Albert crushing on his sister was messing things up somehow? But he couldn't think about that now. It was all too confusing. "Did your visions warn you that this outage was coming?"

"I haven't had a vision in days," she said.

"Are you guys sure this isn't all because of me and Lena?" Marcus asked. "It wouldn't be the first time our powers messed stuff up."

"My dad says it's not possible," Natalie said, but she sounded skeptical.

"What do *you* think?"

"Well…" She smoothed back her long hair. "This started all at once, right? Like something triggered it? So either you guys caused it, or something else did."

At that moment, the door opened, and Ann-Marie stormed onto the porch in her running clothes. She was moving so fast that she crashed right into Natalie, sending the girl stumbling into a potted plant.

"Whoa! Sorry!" Ann-Marie said, pulling Natalie up to her feet. Then she glared at Marcus. "What are you doing lurking out here? Dad said you have to load the dishwasher."

"I should go," Natalie broke in. "I'll let you know if there's any news, okay?" Then she hurried down the steps.

"News about what?" Ann-Marie asked, stretching her hamstrings.

"Nothing." Marcus frowned. "Since when do you go running after dinner?" Normally, his sister woke up at dawn—or even earlier—to go sprinting around the neighborhood.

"They're at it again," she said, motioning toward the house. Sure enough, Marcus could hear his parents' raised voices. "Apparently, Mom was scraping the frying pan the wrong way."

Marcus shook his head. "You ever wonder what changed? I mean, at some point, they must have actually liked each other, right?"

Ann-Marie shrugged. "What's the point? It's not like we can do anything to fix it." Then she gave him one last glance and jogged away into the night.

While Marcus got ready for bed, he couldn't stop thinking about what Natalie had said about something triggering the power outage. As far as he could tell, it had started that morning. At least, that was when he'd noticed his powers not working. Eddie had sent the message about the power outage only an hour later, so it looked as if other people had experienced theirs at the same time.

If Lena and Marcus were to blame, wouldn't their powers have gone out first? And how could this be their fault? Lena wasn't even around for them to have another power-swapping kiss or to be out of tune with each other and make their powers go haywire. Still, Marcus couldn't simply sit back and wait for Eddie to fix things. He needed to do something. But he had no idea where to start.

Instead of hopping into bed, he began looking up world events that had happened that day. But there were no earthquakes or volcano eruptions or UFO sightings, nothing that seemed major enough to have caused this kind of disruption.

At a loss, Marcus moved on to worrying about what to do about Albert, but he came up empty again. He considered calling Lena and asking for advice, but they'd already had their scheduled phone call for the day, and he knew she was busy memorizing her lines. Plus, he'd sent her way more messages than she'd sent him. Any more would make him feel pathetic. He'd wait until the morning.

He wished that Grandpa Joe were still around to offer one of his old-fashioned bits of advice. "Put your head down and keep rowing!" or "You never know what the cat will drag in until you let him outdoors." But he wasn't sure even Grandpa would have much to say in this situation, especially since his grandfather hadn't known about the supernatural part of Marcus's life.

His phone beeped. It was a message from Lena. Just wanted to wish you a good night! Marcus smiled as he read it, his worries easing slightly.

Then there was a knock on the door. "Marcus?" his mom said, poking her head in. "I thought you went to bed."

"I will in a minute. Just looking something up."

He expected his mom to leave, but instead, she came to sit on his bed. "How are you holding up without Lena?" she asked. "It seems like you two have gotten really close."

Marcus shrugged. "Okay, I guess. It stinks not to be able to talk to her whenever I want."

"Your sister said you had a friend stop by tonight? I'm glad you're branching out," his mom said. "It's not good to spend too much time alone." She laughed. "That's how you wind up thinking that sculpting things out of dough is a good idea."

There was a long silence.

"Mom?" Marcus asked softly. "Are you and Dad okay? You guys seem so…off lately."

His mom sighed. "Every relationship has its ups and downs. You've had yours with Lena, haven't you?"

"Yeah, but do you still even like each other?"

In the past, his mom would have brushed off that kind of question, but this time, she took in a deep breath and said,

"Sometimes when you've been with someone for a while, you have to reevaluate how you fit into each other's lives."

"So you don't fit together anymore?" He didn't like the sound of that.

"No, no. Of course we do," she said. "The pieces that made us click together are still there. But the puzzle's changed a little bit, that's all. I think we're just figuring out how to catch up."

"What made you click together when you guys met?" Marcus asked. He'd often wondered about the matchmaker who'd zapped his parents. Whoever it was must have been pretty powerful to take on such a tough job.

His mom smiled. "This might surprise you, but your father and I met at an art gallery. He was there with a friend and didn't know much about art, but he was willing to learn. In fact, when we first started dating, we would even paint together sometimes." She shrugged. "After a while, he got more interested in redoing our kitchen than in helping me splatter-paint bits of old cardboard, but we both love creating things. We always have."

Marcus could hear his father still prying up pieces of tile in the bathroom down the hall, the way he'd been doing all day. He'd assumed his dad took on those kinds of projects to torture the whole family, but if his mom was right, then it was actually his weird way of being artistic. Huh.

"Anyway," his mom went on. "Things will be fine. Don't worry. Now get some sleep, okay? Guaranteed your dad is going to drag you out of bed bright and early tomorrow."

Marcus groaned. "Don't remind me." He turned off his computer and jumped into bed. He was surprised when his mom came to tuck him in, something she hadn't done in years.

"Good night, Marcus," she said, kissing his forehead.

"Good night, Mom," he said as she went out into the hall. Then he snuggled under his covers, feeling a little better than he had a few minutes earlier, and turned off the light.

Chapter 6

Lena tried to focus on learning her lines, but all she could think about was the power outage. Last time her powers had stopped working, she'd had to chase a soul around for days, putting up with its endless practical jokes. She really didn't want to have to worry about finding shaving cream in her shoes again. Besides, was it too much to ask for a week off from that kind of crazy stuff?

Finally, she put her script aside and texted Marcus to wish him a good night. Funny how only a couple of months ago, the two of them had barely been friends, and now it felt strange to go through a whole day without seeing him, let alone a whole week.

With a sigh, she went out to the living room where she found her mom putting on a coat while scrolling through her phone.

"Are we going somewhere?" Lena asked.

"Thanks to the power outage, souls aren't moving on when

they're supposed to. Someone has to track them down." Her mom ran her hand through her hair, which was looking a little limp at the end of the day. "I have three to catch tonight. Hopefully, I can convince them to move on to the After without my powers."

"Okay, let me put my shoes on," Lena said. She didn't know much about soul hunting, but maybe she could help somehow.

But as Lena grabbed her sneakers, her mom stopped her. "You need to get some sleep. I've asked Mrs. Martinez from across the hall to watch you while I'm out."

"Watch me? You mean she's going to *babysit*?"

"I'll feel better if I know someone is here in case of an emergency."

"Mom! I'm old enough to—"

"Please, Lena," her mom said, and the exhaustion in her voice made Lena stop arguing. She'd only been here a day. She didn't want the two of them to be at each other's throats already.

"Okay," Lena said softly. "Good luck."

A knock came at the door, and an ancient woman shuffled in. She was older than anyone Lena had ever met, and considering how many elderly folks Lena had encountered during her soul collections, that was saying a lot.

"This is Mrs. Martinez," Mom said.

"It's nice to meet you," the woman said in a papery-thin voice.

Lena tried to give her a warm smile, but she couldn't help being annoyed. This woman was so old that if there was a fire in the building or something, Lena would have to rescue her and not the other way around.

"Be good," her mom said. She gave Lena a quick kiss and hurried out the door.

After a few awkward moments, Mrs. Martinez had Lena sit on the couch and tell her all about herself, her school, and her friends. The woman nodded and nodded, as if everything Lena said was fascinating. Finally, the old lady's head drooped, and then her soul sparkled inside her chest and slowly rose up until it was hovering above her gray curls. For a terrifying moment, Lena thought she was dead.

But then Mrs. Martinez let out a soft snore, and the soul drifted back down to where it belonged. Lena sighed in relief. Clearly, the woman's soul was a little loose, but it wasn't quite ready to leave its body yet. Lena hoped it wouldn't be for a little while longer.

Once Lena was sure Mrs. Martinez was out cold, she tiptoed into the kitchen to wash the dishes. That would show her mom what a responsible person she was, one who definitely did not need a babysitter! That done, she decided to unpack some of the boxes that her mom still had piled up in the corner of the dining room. After that, she vacuumed and dusted and even rearranged some furniture. Then she hung up the quilt she'd made for her mom for Christmas. Meanwhile, Mrs. Martinez snoozed on.

But as Lena stood in the now-inviting apartment, she couldn't help the restlessness in her stomach. She might have made her mom's apartment feel more comfortable, but Lena wasn't sure it would ever feel like a second home.

Lena woke up in the wee hours to the sound of the front door unlocking. It was just past 5:00 a.m. Had her mom been out hunting souls all night?

She was surprised to see a message from Marcus waiting for her on her phone until she remembered about the time difference. What do you think I should do about Albert? How will I fix him up with someone? Help!

Her mind was still foggy from sleep, but she thought for a second and wrote back: Have you tried using your grandpa's dating book?

When she went out into the hallway, Lena found her mom tiptoeing around, taking off her jacket. Her hair was a mess, and she looked pale and exhausted.

"Are you okay?" Lena whispered, since Mrs. Martinez was

still snoring on the couch. Before she'd gone to sleep, Lena had covered the old woman with a blanket. Mrs. Martinez hadn't even stirred.

"Sorry to wake you," her mom said.

"Did you catch the souls?"

"Two of them," her mom said with a deep sigh. "I'll head back out for the third one later. But I had to come here to shower and change before bringing you to class."

"I could have taken the bus," Lena said, but her mom had wandered into the kitchen to pour herself some water.

"Wow, the place looks great," her mom said after she'd gulped down an entire glass. "I've been meaning to straighten things up for months, but it's been tough to find time to settle in."

"But you are settled, right?" Lena asked. "You want to stay in Phoenix?" For years, her mom had drifted from place to place, barely staying in touch. Now, she'd finally put roots down somewhere. "Because I was thinking that I could come out again over the summer. If you want me to." Maybe things between them would be better if they had more than a week to spend together.

Her mom's tired face lit up. "That would be great! You could stay for the whole summer. Even longer, if you want." She shook her head, her smile dimming. "Hopefully, this whole powers mess will be sorted out by then."

She slumped against the counter, looking ready to fall asleep on the spot.

"Are you hungry?" Lena asked. "I could make you something. Or I could go over to the place across the street and get some bagels."

Her mom's eyes went wide. "You can't go wandering around by yourself in a strange city!"

Lena laughed. "I'd be able to see the apartment the whole time. It's just bagels."

But her mom was vehemently shaking her head. "Absolutely not. It's not safe."

"You said yourself that this is a nice neighborhood. Why can't I—"

"Lena, please. I don't feel like arguing right now." Her mom rubbed her eyes. "It's early. Why don't you go back to bed?"

"I'm still jet-lagged. There's no way I'll get back to sleep."

Her mom glanced down the hall at Mrs. Martinez. "I feel bad waking her, but she can't be comfortable here."

"She seems pretty comfortable to me," Lena couldn't help saying. But she wasn't going to admit that Mrs. Martinez had been sleeping on the job for most of the time. Who knew what kind of person her mom might find to babysit her instead?

Her mom chewed on her lip, a habit that Lena now realized

she had too, thanks to the mirroring exercise they'd done in acting class. "I'll at least cover her with another blanket."

"I'll do it," Lena said. "You go take a shower."

Her mom looked ready to protest, but finally, she nodded and headed off to the bathroom.

Lena's phone buzzed. A message from Marcus. You're a genius! Also, can I wear navy socks with black sneakers?

Hmm, she wrote back, smiling to herself. I'll have to ask Hayleigh. She wasn't sure why Marcus was asking her for fashion advice when all her socks were the same brand and color so that she wouldn't have to worry about matching them. But maybe getting her opinion on things made Marcus feel as though they weren't so far apart.

She tiptoed into the living room and grabbed another blanket. Then she gently placed it on top of Mrs. Martinez. The woman snored and—yet again—her soul drifted out of her body and hovered above her head for a second before dropping back down into her chest.

As Lena took a step back, she was startled to see her own hands suddenly start glowing. Whoa! Her powers were back!

But wait.

As she examined her glowing fingers, Lena realized they weren't glowing the right color. Instead of a deep purple, they were a pale blue. And they weren't simply glowing—they were shining like two spotlights. As if the powers were much stronger than normal. Lena could feel the energy in her hands, like static electricity tingling under her skin.

What on earth? Was this part of the power outage?

Huh. She'd seen this color before. When she'd once begged her mom to call up her soul-hunting powers, the energy coming from her mom's fingers had been that same pale blue.

But that meant...

Lena gasped. Her own soul-collecting powers might have been gone, but somehow she'd gotten her mom's soul-hunting powers instead.

Chapter 7

"What are your likes and dislikes?" Marcus asked, pen at the ready.

"Um, I don't know," Albert said. "Broccoli?"

"You like broccoli or you dislike broccoli?"

Albert seemed to think this over for far too long. "Both. It depends how mushy it is." He frowned. "How are my feelings about broccoli going to get your sister to like me?"

"No idea." Marcus sighed and looked around the mall food court. Grandpa's old dating book advised finding out about the other person's interests to see what the two of you had in common, but so far the only thing Albert and Ann-Marie shared was that they both liked school. Considering they'd been trying to outdo each other for highest GPA for over a year, Marcus didn't think that would exactly bring them together.

His phone beeped. It was a message from Lena. How are things going with Albert?

Marcus sighed and wrote back, Not good. Grandpa's book isn't much help.

"What do you like about Ann-Marie, anyway?" he asked.

Albert's cheeks grew red. "She's…she's so tough. Like the toughest person I've ever met. She doesn't put up with anything from anyone. And she's so smart. I have to work really hard for my grades, but she just gets things."

"She works really hard too," Marcus said. "All she ever does is run and study."

"I don't even have time for extracurricular activities," Albert said. "If I didn't focus on school all the time, I'd never have a chance to beat her."

"Why do you have to beat her? Isn't it better to have a life instead of studying all the time?" Okay, maybe it was ironic for Marcus to be telling someone else to get a life when he'd been pretty much friendless up until he and Lena had started hanging out, but he felt bad for Albert. The guy seemed both excited to have someone to talk to (other than a pet-store parrot) and exhausted to have to use his voice for so many sentences in a row.

Albert nervously cracked his knuckles. "School's the only thing I'm good at. Didn't you ever want to be good at something, really good, so that people would stop thinking you were a joke?"

Marcus could definitely relate to that. It was part of what made him love being a matchmaker. Even though his supernatural identity was a secret from pretty much everyone, at least *he* knew there was something he was good at. Something that made him special.

Another message from Lena. Has he ever tried asking her out?

Good question. But when Marcus posed it to Albert, the guy stared at him in horror.

"What if she says no?" Albert asked.

"Then you'll know." And chances were, she would say no. But at least then Albert could move on.

Again, Marcus realized what a total hypocrite he was being. It had taken him months to ask Lena out, and really, he hadn't even done that in the end. If Connie Reynolds hadn't shoved Lena and Marcus into a closet at her party, he'd probably still be pining after her without actually doing anything about it.

"Hey, how do you feel about parties?" he asked.

Albert nearly spit up his soda. "You mean, like, *going* to one?"

Marcus shook his head. "Never mind."

Negative! he wrote back to Lena.

Okay, he needed a plan. Some way to figure out who Albert's match might be. He seriously doubted it was supposed to be Ann-Marie. "Isn't there anyone else you like? Anyone else you'd want to be matched—er, fixed up with?"

"I thought you said you were going to help me with your sister."

"I did! I, um, I will. But, you know, she's been kind of hanging out with Peter Chung lately, and I don't want you to get your hopes up just in case."

"But they don't have anything in common!" Albert said.

"They're both really into hockey. You should hear them talk about it. They go on and on. It's so boring." In fact, on paper, Ann-Marie and Peter were pretty much perfect for each other. But Marcus couldn't help remembering the distant look on Ann-Marie's face when he'd seen the two of them together at the burger place the day before. And just this morning when he'd told her that Peter had called the house looking for her because she wasn't answering her cell phone, she'd groaned and disappeared into her room. Maybe that meant things between the two of them weren't as rosy as they seemed. Still, that didn't mean Albert was a good match for her either.

You'll figure it out, Lena wrote back. You're a natural at this, remember? Then she sent him an encouraging smiley face that, silly as it was, made him feel a little better.

"Are you sure there's no one else you're interested in?" Marcus asked. "Yesterday at the comic store, was there anyone you noticed? Any cute girls?"

Albert shrugged. "There was a girl I kind of bumped into, but she'd never be into someone like me."

Marcus's body started thrumming with excitement. "When was that?"

"Right before I talked to you. I ran into her on my way into the comic store. I was actually thinking of going back out to find her, but then you came up to me. And then we saw your sister, and well…"

Oh no. Had Marcus messed up his own match? If he'd zapped Albert like he was supposed to, the guy would have gone out to talk to the mystery girl and the two would be matched right now. But since Marcus had been furiously trying to fix the fact that his powers weren't working, he'd kept Albert from talking to the girl again.

"We need to find this girl," Marcus said.

Albert's shoulders slumped. "I don't even know her name!"

"Do you remember anything about her? What did she look like?"

Albert thought for a minute. "Wavy hair. And she was wearing this weird purple scarf with white horses all over it."

Now it was Marcus's turn to almost spit out his soda. "Wait, do you mean *her*?" He grabbed his phone and scrolled through his pictures until he found one from the cast party for the school play.

"I think so," Albert said, frowning at the image. "Her hair was longer, I think, but…yeah, that could be her. Do you know her? Who is she?"

Marcus grinned, an idea forming in his brain. "Her name is Connie Reynolds, and you and I are going to a trampoline park with her this afternoon."

Chapter 8

Lena was ready to burst as she and her mom pulled up in front of the theater for the second day of class. She was dying to tell her about her new powers, but after how her mom had reacted to the idea of Lena crossing the street to get bagels, she wasn't sure how to break the news without her mom instantly panicking. Lena also hadn't told Marcus about the powers yet. The situation was too complex to explain over text message, and besides, he had enough to deal with thanks to the power outage.

"Um, Mom?" she said carefully. "What if I skipped class today and helped you with your assignments instead?"

Her mom's eyes went wide. "You don't like your class anymore?"

"No, it's not that. I just thought...you seem really stressed out. Maybe I could help."

"Honey, that's sweet of you, but my assignments could be dangerous. You could get hurt."

"I'd be careful. And if I'm going to be a soul hunter one day, I should start learning the ropes. Maybe I could read your soul hunter manual to help me get started." *And*, Lena added silently to herself, *to help me figure out what to do about the soul wandering around the theater.*

Her mom shook her head. "Absolutely not. That manual is full of things you're not ready for. I know what I do might sound exciting, but it's not a game, Lena. People die."

"I know that. I'm a soul collector, remember?"

"What Eddie was thinking giving you so much power and responsibility so young is beyond me," her mom said, shaking her head. "It's a miracle you've managed to handle it on your own."

Wait. What? Was her mom saying Lena wasn't up to the job? "Maybe my powers aren't as strong as yours and I haven't had them as long, but I've been doing just fine the past few months."

"You have, and I'm proud of you. I just mean…you don't have to do everything on your own anymore, okay? I'm here to help now." Her mom gave Lena a warm smile. "I'll be waiting here exactly at one. Okay?"

Lena nodded and opened the car door. So much for telling her mom about the power swap. She'd probably lock Lena in a basement to keep her safe.

The first thing Lena noticed when she got into the lobby again was the smell of popcorn. It was much stronger than yesterday, and this time, there wasn't anyone at the concession stand. She glanced around the lobby for any sign of the wandering soul she'd seen the day before, but the place was empty. She couldn't be late to class, but she'd try poking around the building afterward to see if she could find it.

When Lena hurried into the theater, the other kids were already lining up for their aerobic warm-ups. She rushed to join them, relieved to be a couple of minutes early this time.

After they'd done their exercises, Miss Fine had everyone get with their partners to start running their scenes.

"How are you doing with memorizing your lines?" Lena asked Zade.

Zade pulled his script out of his bag. It looked as if it had barely been opened. "I'll get them by Thursday."

"Do you know any of them?" Lena asked.

"Let's see." He launched into the scene without even taking a second to collect himself. Lena mumbled her first line, scrambling to get into character.

As they went back and forth, Zade reading all of his lines, she had to admit that he was a pretty good actor. He might not take acting very seriously, but he had the playful, mischievous Peter Pan thing down. When they got to the part where Wendy was supposed to hand Peter a thimble though, Lena mimed throwing it to him instead. She didn't want to risk bringing her potentially glowing hands anywhere near him.

"Lena!" Miss Fine called out. "This is the moment when Wendy and Peter bond. You need to be closer to him, not all the way on the other side of the stage!"

Lena gulped as she inched closer, still making sure to keep her distance. Above them, the birds in the rafters cooed. They didn't seem to like raised voices.

"Closer!" Miss Fine insisted, coming over. "We need to see that you're learning to trust each other."

But suddenly, Lena couldn't focus on Miss Fine anymore, because the ball of light was back. The soul she'd seen in the lobby yesterday was floating only a few feet away from the stage.

Lena held her breath, waiting for something to happen, but the soul simply hovered in place as if it were content to watch the rehearsal over Miss Fine's shoulder.

"Are you okay?" she heard Miss Fine ask.

"Sorry," Lena said, trying to focus. "Can we start from the top again?"

But as they started the scene over, Lena couldn't concentrate. The light was still hanging there, right behind Miss Fine's head. What did it want?

"Lena!" Miss Fine cried, sounding angry now. "You can't simply stand there. You have to be in the scene!"

Her voice echoed throughout the theater so that the other kids stopped rehearsing to stare at them. Overhead, the pigeons started to stir.

Suddenly, the ball of light dashed over Miss Fine's head and zipped straight at the pigeons. The birds scattered, feathers flying, as if the soul were pushing them off their roost.

A second later—*plop!*—something came from overhead as the scared birds fluttered around. *Plop, plop!* Luis cried out as pigeon poop dripped on his arm, while the other kids ducked for cover.

Meanwhile, the ball of light zipped back out into the audience and then disappeared in the direction of the lobby.

Lena didn't hesitate before running after it.

"Where are you going?" Miss Fine called after her, looking miraculously unscathed, considering the pigeons had been directly above her.

"To the bathroom!" Lena cried. "I'll be right back!"

When she was in the hallway, she found the soul hovering a few feet away by the same "Employees Only" door it had disappeared behind the day before.

"Who are you?" Lena asked. "What do you want?"

"You can see me?" a small voice answered.

Lena glanced over her shoulder as she heard approaching footsteps. Poor Luis was hurrying toward the boys' bathroom, his soiled arm held out in front of him as if it were on fire.

"Follow me," Lena whispered to the soul. Then she rushed to the girls' bathroom. Thankfully, the soul followed her.

When they were safely alone, Lena leaned against one of the sinks, watching the soul hanging in front of a mirror. If anyone came in and heard her talking to herself, she could claim she was practicing her lines.

"I'm Lena. I'm a—a friend. What's your name?"

"Pearl," the voice said.

"What are you doing here, Pearl?" *And why are you scaring pigeons?* Lena silently added.

"I'm here for my friend Myrna."

Lena was surprised to realize that the voice sounded like a girl's. The souls she'd dealt with until this point had all been older, much older. People who'd been sick for a long time and whose time had come to move on to the After. She was willing to bet this soul had been around for a long time. The way the girl talked was a little funny, the way people did in old movies. Maybe she'd been here since the theater was built in the 1930s.

"You mean you're waiting for her?" Lena asked.

The voice didn't answer, but the faded light drew a little closer.

"Well, I'm here to help you," Lena went on. That was true, wasn't it? Having her mom's powers meant she could send souls to the After. It would probably be easier, in fact, since the new powers were stronger. Being a soul hunter couldn't be so different from being a soul collector. And the first thing Lena had learned in her training was that she had to convince Pearl to move on. "What's the last thing you remember, Pearl?"

"The hospital…and Myrna telling me to stay with her," Pearl said. "She always looked out for me."

"What hospital?" Lena asked.

"I…don't remember."

"Do you know why you're here? Why you were drawn to this place?" If Pearl had died at a hospital, then she must have had some personal connection to the theater to now be haunting it.

But Pearl only said, "I miss her. We sang songs together when we were scared."

"When did Myrna leave?" Lena asked. "When was the last time you saw her?"

There was a long silence. "It's been years," Pearl said in a small voice. "Decades, maybe. I don't think she's coming back."

"And do you know that you're…" She couldn't think of a way to phrase the question that didn't sound rude.

"That I'm dead?" Pearl asked. She let out a soft laugh. "Of course I know. All ghosts are dead, aren't they?"

Lena was tempted to point out that there was no such thing as a ghost. There were just souls moving from one place to another, and sometimes, those bits of energy needed a little more time to find where they belonged. But if a soul wanted to call itself a ghost, that was its business.

"I'm here to help you," Lena said.

"Thank you, but I don't need help. I'm doing just fine on my own."

Lena sighed. This was going to be harder than she'd thought. "But you're not meant to be here anymore, Pearl. You're supposed to move on. There's a place called the After. I've heard it's great. I bet you'll see Myrna there."

The bathroom was quiet for a long moment. "You're trying to keep me from doing my job. Others have tried, you know, but it's not going to work."

"No, no," Lena said. "I'm trying to help you."

But the ball of light was backing away, clearly done listening. Suddenly, Lena's hands started glowing. The energy crackled on her fingertips, as if begging to be used. Maybe there was no point in coaxing Pearl to the After with words. Maybe Lena simply had to zap her and send her on her way where she could be at peace.

As Pearl shrunk into the corner, Lena lunged forward and grabbed at the air. Her hand made contact with the soul and—*pow!*—a shower of pale blue sparks scattered across the room.

The energy left her hand, and Lena stumbled back, momentarily blinded by the light. Wow. Her mom's powers really were stronger. Lena couldn't remember ever seeing a shower of sparks like that before.

But as she blinked away the stars from her eyes, she realized something was wrong. The soul—

Lena blinked and blinked, but there was no doubt about it. Pearl's soul was still there, hovering near the ceiling. In fact, the ball of light looked bigger and brighter than before.

"Pearl?" Lena asked. "Why are you still here?" It didn't make sense. The energy had shot out of Lena's fingers and gone into Pearl. That should have sent her to the After.

"What did you do to me?" Pearl asked, her voice suddenly louder.

"I-I don't know," Lena admitted. "You should be gone."

"I feel different." Pearl laughed. "I feel stronger. You're right. You did help me. Now I can do my job even better! Thank you!" Then she let out another laugh and zipped into a nearby air vent, fading like a swirl of smoke.

Chapter 9

On his way to the trampoline park, Marcus decided to ride past Lena's house even though it was completely out of his way. As he left his own neighborhood, Marcus hurried past Caspar Brown's house. The big bully was in the middle of his driveway, punching deflated basketballs. Marcus ducked his head and pedaled as fast as he could. The last thing he needed was yet another run-in with Caspar's fists.

When he got to Lena's house, he paused at the mailbox, shivering in the cold wind. Obviously, Lena wasn't there, and he wasn't sure her dad was even home, but seeing her house made him miss her a little less—and also a little more.

He was desperate to talk to her even if it was nowhere near the time for their scheduled phone call. He knew she was busy with her class and with her mom and stuff, but he couldn't help himself. Not only did he miss Lena like crazy, but with everything going on, he needed someone to talk to, and since Eddie still wasn't answering his phone, and Grandpa was gone,

Lena was the only person he had. Finally, he settled on texting her a bad joke he'd read online the other day. Why do ghosts love elevators? Because they lift their spirits!

Marcus chuckled to himself, imagining Lena groaning and rolling her eyes when she read it. But he hoped she was also laughing and wishing he were there with her. He hovered near her mailbox for another minute before finally heading on his way.

When he got to the trampoline park, he scanned the place for Connie and noticed that everyone seemed to be coupled up. Even some of the employees were holding hands or giggling together. Was there something weirdly romantic about trampolines?

Albert wasn't there yet—Marcus realized he probably should have picked him up to make sure he actually came—but Connie and the other kids from school were already waiting for their turn to jump.

"Marcus, you came!" Connie said, going to hug him again. He wasn't sure he'd ever get used to suddenly being in her circle of friends.

"I hope you don't mind, but I invited a friend of mine to come," Marcus said. "He should be here any second." He was hoping when Connie saw Albert again, sparks would fly with or without Marcus's powers, but there was still no sign of Albert. At least Connie seemed to be the only one here who wasn't part of a couple. That was one point in Marcus's favor.

"Do you know everyone?" Connie asked, motioning to the other kids.

She started doing introductions, but all the couples were so focused on each other that they barely glanced up at Marcus. Among them was Lena's best friend Abigail, giggling with a guy named Ty from Marcus's English class. Marcus didn't even realize the two of them knew each other, and now here they were, acting like the happiest of couples. He was surprised Lena hadn't told him about this, but maybe she didn't know. Considering the bright love sparks around the couple, they'd probably only been zapped in the past couple of days.

In fact, all of the couples seemed to be glowing with love sparks. Were all these pairs newly zapped? Another matchmaker must have been really busy right before the power outage.

"So things are still good with you and Lena?" Connie asked.

Marcus looked at her. "Why, do you know something I don't?"

"No…" Connie cleared her throat. "But my cousin's so busy practicing the piano all the time that she never dates anyone. I think she could use a sweet guy, and I was thinking that I could fix the two of you up. Especially now that she finally let me do her hair!"

Marcus shook his head. "Sorry. I have Lena."

Connie squinted at him. "Yeah, I guess I can see that. You're pretty bright."

"Bright?" Marcus asked. "What do you mean?"

Before she could answer, the door opened, and Albert Landry came in. He looked absolutely terrified to be around so many people rather than locked away in his room studying. Funny how only a few months ago, Marcus had been just as shy and terrified of social situations as Albert was. (Although, to be fair, he'd never resorted to spilling his secrets to a bird.) If Lena hadn't pulled him out of his shell, Marcus would probably still spend most of his time working on his models and doing his best to avoid the outside world.

"You came!" Marcus said, hurrying over to Albert in case he changed his mind and darted back out. He dragged Albert over to the other kids and made sure to plant him directly in front of Connie. "This is Albert," he announced.

Connie gave him a vague smile. "Hey," she said.

Meanwhile, Albert was staring at her, his mouth gaping open. Marcus waited for him to say something, but he didn't. He didn't even seem to be breathing. Wow, he was even worse at talking to girls than Marcus was!

"This is Connie," Marcus said finally. "I think you guys bumped into each other at the mall yesterday."

Connie frowned. "I don't think so…" Then her face lit up. "How old are you?"

"Fifteen," Albert managed to whisper.

"Perfect! How do you feel about girls who play the piano?"

Albert gave her a confused look. "They probably have a good sense of rhythm?"

"Wait," Marcus jumped in. "Are you thinking of fixing him up with your cousin?"

"She's really cute!" Connie said. "Once I convince her to do something about her personality and stuff, she'll be totally dateable." She was grinning like crazy now. "I'll call her and see if she can come meet us! Be right back!"

After she'd dashed off to grab her phone from her purse, Albert seemed to start breathing again. "So where's the girl from the mall?"

Marcus stared at him. "Wait, you mean that wasn't her?"

"Her? She's so loud! And she's wearing way too much perfume."

"But the girl you described, it sounded just like her. The horse scarf and everything!"

Albert fiddled with the leather strap of his watch. "I probably should have told you that I'm kind of face blind."

"Face blind?"

"It means I don't have a good memory for faces. I usually go by voice and clothes and stuff. I recognized you because of your hair and the fact that you smell like rubber cement." He chuckled and then studied Connie again. "But I really don't think that's the girl from the mall."

Marcus's hope evaporated. If Connie wasn't the person Albert was supposed to be matched with, then did that mean Ann-Marie was? It just didn't seem possible.

"Connie's cousin didn't sound too bad," Marcus said weakly as one of the employees waved the group over to some trampolines that had freed up.

"Wait, we're supposed to jump on those?" Albert asked, inching away. "I...I think I should go. I'm not supposed to do anything without a doctor's note."

"This isn't gym class," Marcus said, but Albert wasn't listening.

"I'll see you around, okay?" He started to dash for the door.

"Wait!" Marcus said, rushing after him. "Why don't you... come over tonight? Ann-Marie will be there. Maybe you can finally talk to her." He really had to be desperate if he was inviting people over to his house. But he couldn't let Albert disappear when he still hadn't matched him.

Albert considered this for a second. "Okay, but I can't stay long. I need to get exactly eight and a half hours of sleep a night."

Oh boy. "Yeah, sure. Come over at seven thirty, okay?"

"Should I bring your sister a gift?" Albert asked.

"Flowers always work." At least his grandpa's dating book thought so.

Albert frowned. "Will any flowers beat her champion roses?"

Oops. He had a point. Not only was Ann-Marie an amazing

athlete and student, but she also found time to grow perfect, award-winning roses. "How about some chocolates?" Marcus paused. "On second thought, she won't eat them because of the sugar. How about…" His mind churned. "Kale?" She was always going on about how amazing leafy green vegetables were.

"A bouquet of kale?" Albert asked.

"Sure, why not?" If nothing else, she could dump it in those gross smoothies of hers.

Albert looked skeptical, but he nodded. "I'll wear a tie." Then he rushed over to the door, clearly glad to get out of there.

"Where'd your friend go?" Connie asked, bouncing back over. "My cousin's on her way!"

"Um, he had to go home to…feed his parrot."

"Oh." Connie deflated. "I guess I'll tell her not to come. I thought they'd be a good match though. His cloud was even grayer than hers." She sighed and started to walk away.

"Wait," Marcus said, grabbing her arm. His breath was suddenly heavy in his chest. "What did you say about a cloud around Albert?"

"Nothing. Just talking to myself."

As Marcus glanced around the room again, at all the couples that seemed madly in love, barely paying attention to anyone else, a horrible thought dawned on him.

"Connie," he said softly, "did you do this?"

"Do what?"

"Fix them up. All of them? Did your fingers…" He knew it sounded crazy, but he had to ask. "Did they start glowing, and you touched people with them, and sparks started—"

"Flying all around the place?" Connie broke in, her eyes gleaming. "Totally! I don't know what's happening to me, but it's awesome!"

Chapter 10

T he rest of class was torture. Lena wanted to focus on her scene with Zade, but she couldn't stop trying to make sense of what had happened with Pearl. Instead of sending the soul to the After, Lena's new powers had somehow made it stronger. Clearly, her new abilities weren't as straightforward as she'd thought. And what "job" had Pearl been talking about?

Lena found herself jumping at every sound, afraid Pearl would let her presence be known again, but the theater was silent. Even the pigeons had disappeared to its far corners.

It didn't take Miss Fine long to notice how distracted she was. "Lena, where is that amazing focus from yesterday? I thought you were going to be my star pupil!"

"I'm sorry," Lena said. "I'll do better."

But every time she tried to say Wendy's lines, she felt as if her own voice were coming from miles away. Even Zade seemed annoyed, and he was so laid-back that he'd been happy to eat his yogurt that morning with a pen cap because he'd forgotten a spoon.

Finally, Miss Fine dismissed the class, reminding everyone to work on memorizing lines that night.

Lena sighed in relief and quickly packed up her stuff. She was looking over her shoulder as she walked through the lobby, ready for Pearl to jump out from behind every corner. But there was no sign of her. Maybe the zap *had* worked. It had simply taken a little while for it to kick in.

As she plopped down on a bench to wait for her mom, Lena had almost convinced herself that that was true. She listened to the matinee performers doing vocal exercises and warm-ups inside the theater. Their melodic scales echoed through the lobby. And then, an odd sound joined in. It was the tinkling of a nearby, out-of-tune piano.

Lena scanned the lobby until her eyes rested on the antique piano near the concession stand. There, poised on top of the keys, was a ball of glowing light. Pearl.

Slowly, Lena got to her feet and tiptoed toward her, as if she were creeping up on a wild animal. As she drew closer, for just a second, she thought she heard Pearl's voice singing along with the performers. But as Lena inched closer, she tripped over a loose piece of carpet at the bottom of the stairs.

"Ah!" she couldn't help crying out as she lurched forward. She managed to catch herself on the banister, but when she glanced up, Pearl was already fluttering away. Then she was gone.

Lena sighed and went back to waiting. A moment later, she got a message from her mom. Running late. Be there in six minutes!

Suddenly, Lena was back in fifth grade again, right before her mom had left for good, waiting and waiting for a ride home after school. Back then, Lena didn't have a phone, so she'd had no way of knowing that her mom was running late. Sometimes, she'd start to wonder if her mom was coming at all.

Lena knew now that her mom's soul-collecting job had been partly to blame for all those long waits. But it had been more than that. Her mom had also been crumbling under the pressure of her life, not able to handle anything—her job, her family, even herself.

An alarm went off on Lena's phone, reminding her that it was time to call her dad. Just like with Marcus, she'd scheduled phone dates with her dad so she'd be sure to talk to him every day. He'd been a lot more excited about the idea than Marcus had been, probably because her dad was as much of a planner as she was.

"Is everything all right?" her dad asked when she said hello. "The pitch of your voice seems higher than usual, indicating possible emotional distress." That was her dad's nerdy scientist way of saying she sounded upset.

Lena cleared her throat and tried to make her voice sound more normal. "Fine! The class I'm taking is fun, and the weather here is great. I think I'm just jet-lagged."

"But you're having a good time, right?"

"Totally!" she squeaked. Ugh. So much for sounding like herself.

"I'm glad to hear it," her dad said, thankfully not seeming to notice her chipmunk voice. "So tell me something. Why is it that I keep seeing your boyfriend biking past our house?"

"Marcus? But what's the point? I'm not there anyway."

"Sentimentality makes us act in strange ways," her dad said. "They've done studies on it, in fact."

Lena didn't understand why. If anything, she was the opposite of sentimental. Instead of trying to hold on to the past, she was afraid of it happening again. "Dad, before Mom left, did you have any idea it was going to happen?"

He let out a surprised cough. "No…" he said slowly. "Well, perhaps that's not quite true. I knew she was stressed and unhappy, and there were times when she seemed so far away. I think part of her was already gone." He sighed. "But could I have predicted that it was bad enough to make her decide to leave? No, I don't think so." He paused. "Why do you ask? Are things not going the way you wanted them to with your mom?"

"No, no," she said. "I guess living with her has brought

up some old memories, but no, everything's fine. It's great."
At least, it would be if they could just get through this power
outage thing. "I have to go. Tell Viv I say hi, okay?"

She could practically hear her dad smile over the phone at
the mention of his new girlfriend. At least Lena didn't need to
worry about one of her parents. "Will do," he said. "Take care
of yourself, Munchkin."

Right as Lena hung up, her mom pulled up in front of
the theater.

"I'm so sorry, honey," she said when Lena jumped into the
passenger seat. "My assignment took longer than I thought it
would." She sounded drained, and there was what looked like
grease streaked through her hair.

"But you got the soul, right?"

"Yes. Eventually." Her mom shook her head, and her voice
turned soft and distant. "I don't know how much more of this
I can take, honestly. I have more assignments every day, and
they all seem impossible without my powers."

That's when Lena sensed it, the exact thing her dad had
been talking about. Her mom was in the car with her, and yet,
she wasn't.

"It'll be fine, Mom. Whatever happens, we'll figure it
out, okay?"

Her mom gave her a sad smile. Then she shook her head

again as if to clear it, and when she spoke, her voice was back to normal. "How was class? Anything interesting happen?"

Lena opened her mouth, ready to spill everything about Pearl. But…she couldn't. Because the last thing her mom needed was more stress to make her run again. And if Lena told her about Pearl, she'd have to tell her about the new powers too. So Lena forced a smile onto her face and said, "It was good!"

All Pearl wanted was to find her friend. Who knew? Maybe Myrna was still around. In which case, all Lena had to do was reunite the two of them. That was simple enough. And if that didn't work out… Well, Lena didn't know what she'd do. But she was sure she could handle it on her own.

Chapter 11

"When did this start?" Marcus asked Connie when he was finally able to get her alone. He'd had to stand by and watch as she and the other kids flailed around on trampolines for nearly an hour. He'd been too wound up to focus on jumping. His brain was already doing gymnastics to figure out how Connie could suddenly be a matchmaker. And how she could have powers when everyone else's were gone.

"It started yesterday after I saw you at the mall," Connie said as they stood outside the building waiting for her stepdad to pick her up. Her words tumbled out in a breathless flow. "My cousin went home, because she said she was sick of shopping, so I went to get my nails done. The salon lady was going on and on about how lonely she was, and then this guy came in to deliver water, and he was really cute, and then suddenly my fingers started glowing, and the salon lady totally didn't notice and kept working on my nails, and then the light kind of shot out of my fingers and disappeared into her, and the next thing

I knew, she and the water delivery guy were all into each other and totally forgot I was even standing there!"

"You must have been really freaked out," Marcus said, trying to picture what it would be like to have your powers appear without warning.

"Are you kidding?" Connie said. "It was great! Imagine having the power to fix people up whenever you want."

Marcus didn't have to imagine it. "But you can't fix up whoever you feel like," he said. "It doesn't work that way."

"Sure it does! I've fixed up five couples so far. It would have been six if your friend Albert hadn't left. Do you think he'll give my cousin a chance if I make her promise to throw out her rock collection?"

Marcus almost fell over. Connie had managed to fix up five couples in twenty-four hours? "Connie, listen to me! If you go around zapping people at random, it could totally mess up the order of the universe."

She cocked an eyebrow. "How do you know? Wait…can you do this too?"

There was no way he could deny it. "Yes. Or, at least, I could until a couple of days ago. Then my powers kind of shut off."

"What happened to them?"

"I don't know! Last I heard, everyone's powers were out.

That's why it makes no sense that you can do this…unless…"
Marcus's brain was spinning. "You said this all started right
after you saw me? Maybe my powers aren't turned off. Maybe
you have them."

"Can I keep them?" Connie asked eagerly.

This was a far cry from when Marcus and Lena had swapped
powers and Lena had been ready to do anything to get rid of
them. She'd been convinced that love was fake, just chemicals
in your brain making you do crazy stuff. He'd thought that
was hard to deal with, but this was even worse. He couldn't
have someone running around with his powers and zapping
everyone in sight!

"No, Connie, you can't become a matchmaker whenever
you want. You have to be chosen for it."

"But I *was* chosen, wasn't I? Your powers jumped from you
to me. I bet that means I'm supposed to have them."

Marcus couldn't stop shaking his head. Connie wasn't getting it. "I need those powers. I have assignments to do, and I
can't do them when I can't zap people."

"What assignments?"

"Well, right now, it's just Albert. But I could get another
one at any point."

"So I'll help you," Connie said, as if it was the most obvious
thing in the world. "It'll be fun!"

"It's not supposed to be fun!" Marcus roared.

"Wow, Marcus. Relax!"

But how could he relax? None of this made sense. He tried calling Eddie yet again, but it went straight to voice mail. Marcus quickly left him another message and then turned back to Connie. He had to figure out how to keep her from causing any more trouble.

"Until I hear back from my boss, you have to promise you won't zap anyone else."

"Why?"

"Why? Because you're not supposed to be zapping people at all! That's not how it works!"

"Then how does it work?"

He took a deep breath, realizing he'd been talking so loudly that people in the parking lot were staring. "Okay, let me back up." He tried to explain to her about assignments and auras and the order of things. "If you fix up people who aren't supposed to be together, it won't last. And if you do it for personal gain, then—"

"I get it!" Connie said. "Wow, you make it sound so boring. Maybe these couples won't wind up together forever, but I mean, look at them!" She pointed to Abigail and Ty, who were coming out of the trampoline park holding hands. Even if Marcus hadn't been able to see the sparks around them, he would have still said they were glowing. "When I got here, they looked so blah, so I did the matchy thing, and now they're so happy!"

Marcus sighed. Poor Abigail. Just a few weeks ago, she'd been zapped with a love bolt that had gone crazy, and she and her friend Hayleigh had spent days fighting over a guy who wasn't interested in either of them. Finally, her life had gone back to normal, and here she was again, under yet another love spell. Okay, she did look pretty happy as Ty put his arm around her, but who knew how long that would last? And if they weren't a good match, they'd be even more miserable when it was over.

"They might be happy now," Marcus said, "but that's not up to us to decide. We get assignments, and we do them and—"

"Maybe *you* do, but I'm not like you. I don't have a boss. I don't have to follow anyone's rules."

"But—you—"

"Oops. My ride's here," Connie said. "See you later!"

"No, wait!" Marcus cried. "I need your help with Albert!" If he did finally figure out who the guy was supposed to be fixed up with, it would be a lot easier to do it with powers. Even if they were in the wrong person.

She paused. "When are you supposed to fix him up?"

"He's coming over to my house at seven thirty, so I was thinking I could—"

"Okay. I'll see you then!" Connie called. Then she gave him a wave with her perfectly manicured hand, hopped into her stepdad's car, and zipped away.

Chapter 12

C an you see me okay?" Eddie asked, his face barely visible on Marcus's laptop.

Marcus squinted. "Why is it so dark?" He turned down the volume so that his family members, who were still finishing up dinner while Marcus "worked on his geography project," couldn't overhear the conversation.

"I'm in my basement," Eddie said. "My phone gets no reception here, so I come down when I need quiet."

Was that why Marcus hadn't been able to get Eddie on the phone in days? He'd been hiding in his basement and sending Natalie out to deliver messages? Then again, if tons of people were looking to Marcus for answers, he'd probably be hidden underground too.

"Let's get Lena on the line," Eddie said. He started clicking around, and his face lit up. "Ooh! I can make my voice sound like a robot!" An instant later, he asked, "How is this?" Not only did his voice have a hint of a Spanish accent, but now it was also brassy and mechanical.

"Creepy," Marcus said. "We were going to talk to Lena, remember?"

"Affirmative," Eddie said with a robotic chuckle.

Great. The whole world was messed up, and Marcus's boss was still acting like a little kid. Marcus wasn't sure whether to be annoyed that he wasn't taking things seriously or to see this as a good sign. If the world was about to end, surely Eddie wouldn't be using a drawing pad to sketch robot antennae on the screen right now, would he?

Finally, Lena's face appeared next to Eddie's on Marcus's computer. The instant Marcus saw Lena, he relaxed a little. They'd figured out plenty of crises in the past. Surely they'd be able to figure out this one too.

"Sorry I couldn't get back to you kids sooner," Eddie said. "Things have been crazy."

Lena blinked at his weird robot voice but didn't say anything. Clearly, she was as used to Eddie's antics as Marcus was.

"But you're fixing it, right?" Marcus said. "You figured out why this is happening?"

Eddie let out a long, distorted sigh. "I wish I could say yes, but the truth is, we are stumped. We have never seen this kind of thing before. It seemed to happen overnight."

"And random people have been getting powers all over the world?" Lena said. "It's not just us?"

"Us?" Eddie said. "You have been experiencing power swaps too?"

"What?" Lena blinked rapidly. "No. I just meant Marcus and Connie. But if it happened to them, it could happen to anyone, right?" Her voice was oddly high-pitched, and Marcus had the feeling she was lying. But why would she hide something from Eddie?

Their boss didn't seem to notice though, as he continued, "I am afraid it's happening everywhere. Thankfully, it appears temporary. Some of the powers have already faded."

"Oh phew," Marcus said. That meant Connie might not be a matchmaker for much longer. Who knew how many more couples she'd zapped since he'd seen her? He'd tried texting her to remind her *not* to use her new powers, but she only sent back a bunch of smiley faces.

"But why is this happening at all?" Lena chimed in. "If our powers are gone, how could they be jumping to other people?"

"They're not gone, not completely." Eddie scratched at his short beard. "Think of your powers like a web. They're all connected to each other. But for some reason, that web snapped, and strands went all over the place. Now, they are hanging loose, and sometimes, they will latch on to someone else for a little while. But then that thread will snap back and hang loose again."

"So how do we patch up the web?" Lena asked.

Eddie shook his head. "It is not like a quilt. Patching will do no good. It needs to be rebuilt."

"But how?" Marcus asked.

Eddie sighed. "That I don't know."

"Natalie and I were thinking that if we can trace the source of the outage, we might be able to—"

"We have already tried that," Eddie broke in. "There is no event that seems significant enough to have caused this."

"And you're sure it's not our fault somehow?" Marcus asked.

"How can it be?" Lena jumped in. "I'm not even there."

Something clicked in Marcus's head. "Wait, what if that's the reason? I mean, things went crazy right around the time Lena left town, didn't they?"

Eddie looked skeptical. "I have worried about the link between your powers being so strong and causing further problems. But Lena leaving town, it is such a small thing…"

"Our powers have been linked ever since we swapped them, right?" Marcus asked, his brain spinning. "It's caused chain reactions before. Why couldn't it cause something bigger?"

"I can look into it," Eddie said, but despite his mechanical voice, he sounded doubtful. Then Eddie gave them a robotic send-off—"Beep beep boop"—and the shadowy screen went completely black, leaving Lena and Marcus alone in the video chat.

Marcus could see how worried she looked. "Are you okay?"

She sighed. "This is not the relaxing vacation with my mom that I was imagining."

"I know what you mean. I haven't worked on a single model so far. But we'll figure this out, okay? Did you get the elevator joke I sent you?"

Her face brightened. "Yes, you cheeseball!" She chuckled. "Where do you come up with this stuff?"

"It's amazing what you find when you look up 'ghost jokes.'" He expected Lena to correct him, since she was not a fan of the word "ghost." But her expression was far away, and she was worriedly chewing on her lip. "Hey, what's going on?"

Lena shook her head. "There's just a lot happening. I need to work on my lines before tomorrow, and I have to do some research about a soul that's haunting our theater, and—"

"A soul at the theater? You didn't tell me about that."

She sighed. "Yeah. And…" He could see her wrestling with something. Finally, she added in a whisper, "Don't tell Eddie, but I think I have my mom's powers. I'm trying to use them to get rid of this soul, but it's not going that great so far."

"Whoa!" Marcus cried. "How did that happen? What does your mom say? And why can't I—"

"She doesn't know about the soul yet, which is why I don't want Eddie to know either. I'm trying to figure it out on my own."

"Are you sure it's a good idea to keep it a secret?"

"Trust me. My mom can't handle any more stress right now. I'll tell her when things calm down a little."

"Maybe I could help. I'll try looking some stuff up for you or—"

"That's okay. You have enough going on." She smiled, her face softening. "But thank you. I'll let you know if I need help."

"You want me to call you later? I could—"

"Sorry. I have a phone call scheduled with Hayleigh in a minute. She's freaking out about Abigail's new boyfriend. I'll talk to you tomorrow, okay?" She smiled and added, "Beep beep boop." Then she was gone.

Lena couldn't help feeling guilty as she hung up the phone. It was obvious that Marcus had wanted to keep talking to her, but she couldn't focus on joking around with him when there was so much to worry about. She'd call him tomorrow. Once she'd done some research on Pearl.

She'd just managed to look up the theater and connections to anyone named Pearl or Myrna—with no results—when her phone rang.

"Abigail is driving me insane!" Hayleigh cried. "She only wants to hang out with Ty all the time. A couple of days ago, she'd never even mentioned him, and now, she won't stop talking about him. What am I supposed to do?"

"Give it a few days," Lena said. "I bet it'll blow over." Once Connie's love boost faded, chances were Abigail and Ty would realize they had nothing in common.

"I don't want them to break up!" Hayleigh said. "I want to double-date with them!"

"Uh-oh. Does this mean you're into someone new?" Lena asked. Her friend was always developing enormous crushes on guys and then getting her feelings hurt over and over.

"No, but I'm sick of being alone," Hayleigh said. "I know not all of us can find our perfect matches like you and Marcus, but that doesn't mean I can't have some fun dating, right?"

"There's no such thing as a perfect match," Lena said. "Everyone has their problems."

"Wait. Don't tell me there's trouble in Lena and Marcus paradise!"

"No, not trouble," Lena said slowly. "Marcus is great. I mean, ever since I landed in Phoenix, I keep taking pictures of things I know he'll like and trying to remember stuff that I want to tell him. But he keeps acting like I'm still home, calling me and texting me all the time for advice on stuff. Of course I like hearing from him, but...but I have my own life too. You know?"

"Did you tell him that?"

"I can't. He'll take it so personally."

"Aw, poor Marcus!" Hayleigh said. "He's getting the Lena cold shoulder."

"The what?"

Hayleigh giggled. "Just something Abigail and I used to say, back when you always pretended that stuff didn't bother you. You've gotten a lot better about having actual emotions since you and Marcus got together."

"I'm not giving anyone the cold shoulder!" Lena said.

"Not on purpose, but remember when I broke up with Eli last summer during camp, and I cried about it every day for, like, a week?"

"Um, yeah, vaguely," Lena said, trying not to laugh. Hayleigh had been consumed by that whole drama for weeks. As far as Lena could tell, Eli hadn't even realized that he and Hayleigh were dating until she'd suddenly broken up with him on the last day of camp. At which point it had turned out that Eli hadn't even known Hayleigh's name. "What about it?"

"Abigail was totally there for me to cry on her shoulder and stuff, but you…" She chuckled. "You gave me a package of name tags and said that next year, I should wear one all through camp so the guy I like will know my name."

"So?"

"So!" Hayleigh cried on the other end. "That is not a normal thing to do, Lena!"

"Why not? I saw you were upset, and I came up with a way to help you."

"So that you wouldn't have to listen to me cry anymore," Hayleigh said. "And it's fine. I get it. I didn't take it personally, because I knew that's how you were about other people and their emotions. But Marcus is still figuring you out. What if he doesn't know that yet?"

Lena laughed. "Trust me, Marcus knows more about me than anyone else. And I'm not giving him the cold shoulder. Like you said, I'm different now. Being with Marcus has totally loosened me up. I'm not shutting anyone out."

"If you say so," Hayleigh said. It was clear she wasn't convinced.

>>>— Chapter 13 →

When the doorbell rang that night, Marcus was ready. He'd furiously cleared away as much of his sister's workout equipment as he could and sprayed the whole house with air freshener to cover up the smell of moldy bread. The place still reeked, but at least the mold smell was a little more flowery now. He wasn't sure what his sister would say when she came home from the gym to see and smell what he'd done.

He pulled the door open, expecting Albert, and found Connie's excited face grinning back at him instead. "Okay, where is he?" she asked, brushing past him. "Let's get this whole zapping thing over with. I just saw someone else I want to fix up."

"Whoa, keep your voice down!" Marcus hissed. His dad was out getting more supplies for the bathroom, but his mom was in the basement, still working on her sculptures. "This is supposed to be a secret, remember? And we're not zapping Albert. We don't even know who he's supposed to be fixed up with.

He has a crush on my sister, but I really don't think she likes him back."

"Why not just zap her and Albert and see what happens?"

"Because it doesn't work that way, okay?" Marcus practically yelled. "Besides, she's already hanging out with this guy Peter Chung."

Connie shrugged. "Fine. But if we're supposed to make Albert dateable…" She scrunched up her nose. "We're going to need some help." She whipped out her phone and started typing.

"What are you doing?" Marcus asked.

"Calling for reinforcements."

Ten minutes later, Albert arrived, exactly on time, wearing a bow tie and clutching a clump of kale tied with a ribbon. He looked downright petrified at the sight of Connie. "Marcus, where's your sister?" he whispered, glancing around.

"Working out. She should be home soon."

Albert looked both disappointed not to be able to see Ann-Marie and relieved that he wouldn't actually have to talk to her yet.

The doorbell rang again, and Lena's other best friend, Hayleigh, burst in. She was panting as she lugged in a giant sparkly bag. "I heard there was a makeover emergency!" she cried. Then she glanced at Albert, and her face lit up. "Oh! I see. Let's get to work."

"Makeover?" Albert whispered, looking ready to leap behind the couch for cover.

"You want girls to notice you, right?" Connie asked.

Albert could barely look at her as he gave a feeble nod. Then he glanced at Marcus as if looking for reassurance. "It'll be fine," Marcus found himself saying.

Soon, Hurricane Connie had swept Albert into Marcus's bedroom, and she and Hayleigh started circling around him, talking about his shoes and his clothes and even his nose hair! As they snipped at his unruly locks and made him try on Hayleigh's brother's old sweaters, Marcus could only stand back and watch, thankful that Lena had never subjected him to anything so terrible. When they were done, Marcus had to admit that Albert looked good. He was like a cleaned-up version of himself.

"How do you feel?" Marcus asked him. Then he squinted. "Is that glitter in his hair?"

Hayleigh giggled. "Sorry. I couldn't help myself. But it'll wash out. I promise!"

Albert stared at himself in the mirror for a long while. "You think Ann-Marie will like it?" he asked finally.

"Of course she will," Connie answered. "When you see her, you should ask her to the New Year's Eve dance. It'll be so much fun!" She turned to Marcus. "Have you convinced Lena to come back for it yet?"

He shook his head. "I haven't really talked to her lately." At least not about that kind of nonmagical thing.

Hayleigh giggled and gave an exaggerated eye roll.

"What?" Marcus asked.

"Nothing," she said, but she was still fighting a smile. "Last time I talked to Lena, she said you're always calling her and stuff. It sounds like all you do is talk to her."

"It's sweet," Connie broke in. "Really. But girls don't like to feel smothered, you know?"

"I'm not smothering her! We just have a lot of…" Marcus shook his head. "You wouldn't understand. But she likes it when I check in."

Hayleigh only gave him a knowing smile, and Marcus felt his cheeks growing hot. Is that what Lena had been telling her friends? That he was smothering her? With everything going on with their powers, he'd needed someone to talk to. Besides, she was his girlfriend. Didn't that mean she wanted to talk to him as much as he wanted to talk to her?

Just then, the front door opened, and they heard Ann-Marie stomp in.

Connie turned to Albert. "Ready to go wow her with your new look?"

Albert nodded and squared his shoulders. Maybe this makeover was a good idea after all. He seemed a little surer of himself as he tugged at his sleeve and held up the kale bouquet.

Marcus tried to give him an encouraging nod, even though he wasn't sure this was the best idea. But Hurricane Connie was picking up even more speed. He figured it was best to go along with it and hope that by some miracle her plan worked.

While Hayleigh and Connie eavesdropped from down the hall, Marcus and Albert went out into the living room.

Ann-Marie jumped at the sight of them. "Oh, I didn't know anyone was home," she said, smoothing back her sweaty hair as she frowned at Albert. "What are you doing here? And what are you wearing?"

"This is for you," Albert said, holding out the bouquet.

She took a step back. "Is that kale?"

"You put it in your smoothies all the time, right?" Marcus jumped in.

"It's a good source of folic acid," Albert said. "It boosts brain development."

Ann-Marie shook her head. "Whatever. I have to go take a shower."

"Dad said no showers," Marcus chimed in. "He had to disconnect the water."

"Are you kidding me?" His sister groaned and started to push past them.

"Ann-Marie, wait!" Albert croaked. She stopped. "I was wondering...if you would...go to the...New Year's Eve dance...*avec moi.*" He blinked. "I mean, with me." He blinked again and again. "I don't know why I just said that in French. Wait. I'm not speaking French right now, am I?"

"You're asking me to a dance?" Ann-Marie said, her eyes wide.

"*Oui,*" Albert said. "I mean *sí.* I mean yes."

After that display, Marcus was sure his sister would shoot poor Albert down, so he almost stopped breathing when Ann-Marie shrugged and said, "I'll...think about it." She started toward her room, but then she paused and added, "By the way, Albert. I, um, I like your hair that way." Then she rushed out of the room. A second later, they heard her bedroom door slam shut.

Albert's face was absolutely on fire as he turned toward Marcus. "Did she just pay me a compliment?" he asked in disbelief. "And does that mean she might actually go to the dance with me?"

Marcus nodded, also kind of in shock. Then he glanced at Connie, who was sashaying over to him, Hayleigh practically skipping behind her down the hall.

"I told you I knew what I was doing!" Connie said. "Now will you finally listen to me?"

Marcus sighed. He supposed he didn't have a choice but to get out of Hurricane Connie's way.

Chapter 14

When Lena's mom dropped her off at the theater early the next morning, Lena set out to track down Pearl. She prowled around the building, poking her head into every room she could find, but besides some startled squirrels and an angry pigeon, she didn't find anything.

Her research the night before had also come up empty. Besides looking into the theater's history, Lena had also searched patients named Pearl and Myrna at nearby hospitals but hadn't had luck with either. She had found some of the stuff Shontelle had mentioned on the first day of class about past performances at the theater getting canceled or delayed. Lena suspected those had something to do with Pearl's "job." Whatever Pearl was after, Lena was not going to let it mess up this show too.

"Lena, you're here early," Miss Fine said when they bumped into each other in the lobby.

"Um, yeah, I wanted to apologize for being so distracted yesterday."

"We all have off days." Miss Fine laughed, the strict persona fading away a little. "Well, except for my mother. She was the luckiest person I ever knew. Sometimes, I wish I'd inherited some of her luck."

Lena tried to smile, but at that moment, she was wishing she hadn't inherited quite so many things from her mom. Their shared love of acting was okay, but the whole soul-collecting thing was getting to be a real pain.

"I also wanted to talk to you about something," Lena said slowly. "You probably noticed that I don't like getting too close to people and touching them and stuff."

"I did pick up on that yesterday," Miss Fine said, nodding.

"I kind of have a thing about germs." She figured that was a believable excuse. Definitely more believable than "I could kill someone with my glowing fingers."

Miss Fine gave her an examining look, but she didn't ask any questions. "Thanks for letting me know," she said instead. "Just do the best you can, okay?"

Lena nodded. That was the plan.

When they got in the theater and other kids started trickling in, Miss Fine was all business again. "All right, everyone. Let's do your exercises, and then we'll run scenes. I hope you know your lines! We'll do some drills later to help you remember them."

Zade gave Lena an eye roll and whispered, "Drill sergeant."

She couldn't help smiling. Yes, Miss Fine was like a drill sergeant, and this class was like theater boot camp. But that's exactly what Lena wanted. If only the supernatural part of her life would leave her alone, she might actually be able to enjoy it.

As she and Zade ran through the scene, Lena was careful not to get too close to him again. Zade didn't even seem to notice. For some reason, he was busy doing the role of Peter Pan as if he were part monkey. It didn't make any sense with the scene, but it was entertaining to watch. Lena was trying to focus on making every part of her body feel Wendy-like, but when Zade started scratching his armpits, she couldn't help laughing.

"Zade!" Miss Fine called, coming over to them. "I appreciate your energy, but no clowning around, all right?"

"But isn't that the whole point of acting, to have fun with the stuff we're doing?" he asked.

"There's a time and place for that," she said, "but you also have to be true to your character."

"Maybe that's what I'm doing."

Miss Fine crossed her arms in front of her chest. "Peter Pan is a monkey?"

Zade grinned. "Who knows? Maybe that's why he's always zipping around. He's a flying monkey."

A couple of the other kids chuckled, but Miss Fine didn't look amused. "I need you to focus, okay? The showcase is in three days."

Zade didn't look happy, but when they went back to running the scene, he played it straight this time. Lena had to admit that while the scene made more sense when Peter Pan wasn't shoving bananas in his mouth, it also wasn't nearly as much fun.

After a while, Miss Fine lined all the kids up on the edge of the stage and told them to start spouting their lines whenever she pointed to them and to stop saying them when she took her hand away. It only took a couple of rounds of that for Zade to start looking like he might throw a monkey-sized fit. Every time Miss Fine pointed to him, he scrambled to remember his lines and came up empty.

"You were supposed to know them by now," Miss Fine scolded.

"I do!" Zade insisted. "This is just too much pressure."

"If you knew them well enough, this exercise would be easy."

"Miss Fine," Lena couldn't help breaking in. "He really does know them. He was doing great during our rehearsal."

"Then show me," she said to Zade.

Zade blew out a frustrated breath. "Forget it."

"Excuse me?"

"I'm going to get a drink of water," he announced. Then he started to march off the stage. Lena couldn't blame him for being upset, but stomping away like a baby wasn't helping.

"Zade!" Miss Fine called after him. "Come back here!"

He ignored her. Instead, he threw himself into the front row of seats and grabbed some water out of his bag.

Miss Fine looked at a loss. Lena could tell she wasn't used to being disobeyed.

"Zade—" she tried again as he took a few angry swigs from his bottle.

At that moment, Lena spotted a ball of light zipping into the theater. It was heading straight at Zade.

"Pearl, no!" Lena started to cry out, but it was too late.

The light disappeared under Zade's seat and—*pop!*—the chair folded up and tossed Zade out onto the floor, catapult-style. He cried out as he hit the carpet and rolled onto his side.

Lena tore over to him as Pearl retreated into the wings.

"Zade! Are you okay?"

"I'm fine," Zade said with a chuckle, getting to his feet. He flexed his wrist. "I landed on my arm weird, but I think it's okay."

"You're sure you're all right?" Miss Fine asked, rushing over.

"That's what I get for being a monkey boy, I guess," Zade said with a grin.

To Lena's surprise, Miss Fine didn't push the issue. Instead, her face was full of concern. She turned to everyone and called out, "Let's take a break."

"It was like the seat spit me out," Zade said, still rubbing his wrist. "Maybe I taste bad."

"Or maybe it's the ghost," Shontelle said, her eyes gleaming. "I told you this place was haunted."

The other kids laughed, and even Zade joined in. But Lena wasn't laughing. She didn't know what Pearl's deal was, but she'd tried to hurt Zade. Lena had to find a way to send her to the After. And she had to find it soon.

That afternoon, while her mom was in the basement doing laundry, Lena quickly searched the apartment for her soul-hunting manual. If she could find where her mom kept it, she could use it to figure out what to do about Pearl. She couldn't zap her again and risk making her even stronger.

But there was no sign of the manual anywhere. Instead, there were a lot of unpacked boxes and things that had been thrown haphazardly into the closet and behind furniture, as if her mom had meant to finish unpacking but never got around to it.

Lena was scrambling to put her mom's shoes back under the

dresser the way she'd found them when she heard her mom's voice. She was on the phone.

"I can be there in about a half hour. Let me see if my neighbor can watch Lena again. Send me the address, okay?"

Lena rushed out into the living room. "Do you have another assignment?"

Her mom sighed and nodded. "A soul's wandering around in a yoga studio. It won't stop unrolling the mats."

"Let me come with you," Lena said.

"Absolutely not. We already talked about this. It's too dangerous."

"Isn't it dangerous for you to be going out on assignments alone when you don't have your powers?" Lena asked. "Aren't I allowed to worry about you too?"

Her mom shook her head. "You're staying here, and that's final."

When her mom went across the hall to ask Mrs. Martinez to babysit, Lena quickly glanced at her mom's phone and memorized the address Yvonne had sent over.

Five minutes later, Mrs. Martinez was nestled on the couch, asking Lena the exact same questions about school and her family as she had the night before.

Lena wanted to scream. She had to find a way to follow her mom and see her in action. Maybe that would give her some idea of how to handle the Pearl situation.

It was only late afternoon, but Lena pulled down the shades

and insisted on making Mrs. Martinez some warm milk. Then she launched into the most boring story she could think of, about a quilt she'd worked on last summer. As she described different patterns and stitches, the old lady's eyelids drooped. Soon, she was snoring away, and Lena's fingers were tingling again, ready to flare to life as the old woman's soul danced above her gray curls.

This time, Lena made sure to keep her distance, and her new powers calmed down. She left a note on the kitchen table, saying she'd gone to the store for some more milk, in case Mrs. Martinez woke up and panicked that Lena was gone. The odds of that happening were pretty slim though. Her snores were practically shaking the entire building.

When she looked up the address she'd seen on her mom's phone, Lena realized it was too far away to walk, but she didn't have time to figure out how to get there by bus. Then she remembered a bike she'd seen tucked behind some boxes in her mom's bedroom. She dragged it out and checked the tires. The air in the front one was a little low, but it would have to do. She knew her mom would freak out if she saw Lena riding a bike through Phoenix alone, and maybe it wasn't the best of ideas, but she was desperate.

After a long ride in the dry heat, she got to the yoga studio. When she peered in through the window, she saw that class was in session and that her mom was in the back of the room, doing her best downward dog. She was by far the youngest person there—most of the other participants looked like grandparents—but also one of the least flexible.

As her mom stretched her entire body, she looked so peaceful that, for a second, Lena wondered if she'd decided to forget about her assignment and enjoy the class instead. But then she noticed her mom squinting intently at something in the corner of the room, and when Lena looked harder, she could see a small ball of light there. A soul. She watched, rapt, as her mom got to her feet and headed to the corner, pretending that she needed to drink some water. Then she seemed to whisper something to the soul. Lena was dying to know what her mom was saying, but how could she get closer?

Through the window, she spotted a side door next to where her mom was now pretending to stretch her neck while everyone else in the class was sprawled out on the floor. Maybe if Lena could peek through that door, she could see what her mom was doing.

She hurried around to the side of the building in time to see a clump of light shooting out through the door. The runaway soul. That meant Lena's mom would be right behind it.

Lena dove out of sight behind a row of recycling bins just as her mom threw open the door and hurried outside. She scanned the alley, looking for the soul, but she clearly couldn't see it from where she was standing. Lena, though, had a great view of it as it curled under a nearby windowsill. Even though it was only a ball of light like Pearl, it didn't look (or feel) exactly the same. The light was a slightly deeper gold color, and the edges of the soul didn't look as wispy as Pearl's did— another sign that Pearl's soul had been around for a long time.

Her mom glanced around the alley one more time, and then she started to head away from the street. In the wrong direction. Uh-oh.

Thinking fast, Lena grabbed an empty soda can from one of the bins and tossed it a few feet in front of her. The can clanged on the pavement, making her mom spin around. She rushed toward the source of the sound just as the soul unpeeled itself from under the window.

"Stop!" Lena's mom said. "Eleanor, please. I can help you see your husband again."

At those words, the soul stopped moving. "Kevin?" a tiny voice said.

"He's waiting for you," Lena's mom said. "You only have to stop running away. I know you feel at peace here, but where you're meant to go is more peaceful than any yoga class. You'll love it there."

The soul inched forward. "Kevin always said I needed to relax."

Lena's mom smiled. "Imagine the two of you sitting on the beach together, looking out at the ocean, without a care in the world."

The soul stopped moving. "Kevin can't go to the beach."

Lena saw her mom hesitate. "Or somewhere else. Somewhere you both can unwind."

But it was clearly too late. Lena's mom had lost her. "Kevin's not supposed to spend too much time outside. His skin is too sensitive to the sun. That's what got him, you know. Skin cancer."

"I'm sorry," Lena's mom said. "But he's okay now. He's waiting for you. If you just let go—"

"Why should I trust you?" Eleanor asked. "My Kevin always said I was too trusting."

"It's all right. Really. I'm only here to help you."

But Eleanor wasn't listening anymore. She was inching farther away, backing up toward the very bins where Lena was hiding.

Suddenly, Lena's fingers flared to life with pale blue energy. The powers didn't seem to need her help; they knew exactly what to do. The energy shot out of her fingers, wove in between the bins, and wrapped itself around Eleanor's soul. There was a blinding flash, and then the ball of light vanished.

Lena let out a long breath. The soul was gone. She was sure

of it. Unlike with Pearl, there had been no shower of blue sparks. Plus, the relief that now flooded her body was how Lena normally felt when her assignment was complete, though she was usually much more exhausted afterward. This time, she was ready to do it all over again.

When she peeked around the bin, she saw her mom still standing there, looking puzzled. She moved to inspect the spot where Eleanor had been. Lena dove on the ground and tried to make herself invisible.

After a minute, her mom must have been satisfied that Eleanor was gone, because she took out her phone. "Yvonne? It's Jessica. Listen, I got the soul at the yoga studio, but... something seemed off. It looked like she was going to get away again, and then suddenly, she crossed over." There was a long silence. "I'm not complaining, but it seemed a little too easy." She laughed. "I'm just glad I get to go home and have dinner with my daughter instead of chasing this one around all night."

Lena sucked in a breath. Oh no. Her mom was heading home, and Lena wouldn't be there when she got back. As her mom headed the other way down the alley, Lena crept out from the bins. Then, with a glance over her shoulder, she ran to the bike, jumped on, and started furiously pedaling home.

Chapter 15

"Jealousy," Connie said, plopping down on Marcus's couch. "It works every time."

Marcus sank into an armchair and gently placed his grandpa's dating guide on the coffee table. "Not according to this book. It says jealousy is a negative tactic that you should try to avoid."

Connie rolled her eyes. "That book is also about a million years old. Trust me. If you want to fix Albert up with your sister, you need to make him and Peter jealous of each other."

"But we don't even know if Ann-Marie is supposed to be matched with either of them." Until last night, Marcus would have said there was no way his sister and Albert were compatible, but after how Ann-Marie had acted, he wasn't sure what to think anymore. Maybe Connie really did know what she was doing.

"It doesn't matter," Connie said. "It seems like she could like both of them. So let them fight it out, and see which one wins."

Marcus sighed. It seemed cruel to pit the two guys against each other, especially when one of them was afraid of the sound of his own voice. But maybe Connie had a point. Maybe the reason Ann-Marie and Peter hadn't been matched yet was because Ann-Marie had feelings for more than one person.

"Or you could just let me zap someone," Connie added. "That'll solve everything."

"It won't!" Marcus insisted. "If we pick the wrong guy, it'll all fall apart anyway, and they'll all be miserable."

"Okay then," Connie said. "Let's go with my plan."

"Fine. We can give it a try. But how do we get the two guys to fight over her?"

Connie grinned. "I have some ideas."

The gleam in her eyes was a little unnerving. Marcus enjoyed his job, of course, but for Connie, it was clearly more than that. She didn't seem to care how anything actually worked. She hadn't asked Marcus any questions about his powers or about other matchmakers. He hadn't told her about Lena being a soul collector, since he wasn't sure he could trust her with the information. Really, he didn't know if he could trust Connie at all.

"You haven't matched anyone else, have you?" he asked.

"Don't worry about it." Connie waved her hand, as if she were trying to pull a Jedi mind trick on him.

"What does that mean? Have you matched people or not?"

She rolled her eyes. "You said you didn't want to know."

"No, I said you shouldn't do it at all!"

But Connie was already focused on listing ways they could make Peter and Albert compete for Ann-Marie's attention. "A duel could work, but that's a little clichéd."

"A duel? Like with swords?" Marcus said.

"Or pistols at dawn. Some people find that kind of thing romantic."

Ugh. This was not helping. And the longer Albert went without a match, the more messed up the balance of the universe would get. Add that to all the other supernatural jobs that weren't getting done because of the power outage and, well... Marcus didn't want to think about it. The idea was too overwhelming and scary. He'd started leaving the room whenever his dad watched the news, because he couldn't help thinking every bad thing happening in the world was due to the power outage.

"Whatever you do, it has to give the two guys a fair shot, okay?" Marcus asked. "I mean, Peter is this laid-back popular guy, and Albert is...not."

Before Connie could answer, the basement door opened, and Marcus's mother came up, bringing a cloud of moldy dough scent with her.

"Oh, hello," his mom said, giving Connie a startled look. "Marcus, I didn't realize you had a friend over."

He could tell she was surprised he had company for the second time that week, given his track record of absolutely never bringing anyone over to the house.

Before Marcus could do introductions, Marcus's dad burst out of the bathroom holding a severed pipe. "Out of my way!" he hollered, barreling past them with the rusty, leaking monstrosity. Behind him, water was trickling out of the bathroom and onto the hallway floor.

"What happened?" Marcus's mom cried as he ran for the front door.

"I'll fix it!" his dad shouted from the porch.

Marcus's mom huffed and then marched outside, slamming the door shut behind her. A second later, Marcus could hear his parents arguing. Again. Couldn't they at least pretend to get along during the one time he actually had a friend over? (Or whatever Connie was.)

"Is everything okay?" Connie asked.

"Um, yeah," Marcus said. "They're just, um…" He didn't know how to finish that sentence.

"My parents used to fight all the time too," she said softly.

"Did they ever stop?"

"Kind of. They split up and both married other people, and they're a lot happier now." She let out a soft laugh. "If they were still together, I'd probably try to zap them."

"Connie, you can't—"

"Yeah, yeah, I know." She sat back in her seat. "Zapping people isn't the answer to everything. But when you see someone who's miserable, you want to do something about it, right?"

Marcus couldn't argue with that.

Just then, Ann-Marie burst through the front door. Her slumped shoulders told him that his parents were still arguing outside. "Oh." She froze at the sight of Connie.

"I was just going," Connie said, grabbing the list and shoving it in her bag.

"You were?" Marcus asked. "But what about—"

"Don't worry. I know what to do." She gave him a sparkling smile. "No swords or pistols, I promise. Just come to the Y tomorrow afternoon, okay?"

Marcus wanted to press, but Connie only gave him a little wave and headed out the door. Too late, he realized that she'd have to pass right by his parents who were still out on the porch arguing. Great.

He strained to hear and was relieved when his parents' voices died down. At least they had the decency to stop chewing each other out while Connie was walking by.

"What are they fighting about now?" Ann-Marie asked, wiping her forehead with a towel. "I heard Mom say something about a flood?"

Marcus pointed down the hall where the rusty water had finally stopped trickling out of the bathroom.

"Gross," Ann-Marie said. "Maybe when this whole renovation thing is done, they'll stop yelling at each other all the time."

"Maybe," Marcus said, but the truth was, this had started well before his dad tore up the bathroom. In fact, Marcus wondered if part of the reason his dad had started the project in the first place was to focus on something other than all the stuff he and Marcus's mom didn't agree on.

Marcus grabbed a few dish towels from the kitchen and tossed them on the wet hallway floor, but it didn't do much good. No doubt his dad would come in and yell at him for doing it wrong anyway, even though he was the one who'd made a pipe burst in the first place. Still, letting the dirty water seep into the carpet couldn't be good.

"Hey," he called to Ann-Marie, "can you grab some more towels?"

There was no answer.

"Ann-Marie?" he tried again, peering down the hallway. She was standing by the coat rack, staring into space and not moving.

Marcus frowned. His sister not moving was like her not breathing. She was always doing something—stretching, squatting, flexing—to keep her muscles going.

"Are you okay?" Marcus called out to her. As he took a step

closer, he saw that her eyes were open, but they were empty. She was so still that she could have been made out of marble.

And then her eyelids fluttered, and she was back.

"Marcus?" she said in confusion, as if coming out of a dream.

"What happened? Are you okay?"

"I don't know," she said. "I think I just saw… But that's impossible. It couldn't have been…"

And that's when something clicked in Marcus's brain. He'd witnessed this before. When he'd watched Natalie having one of her visions, she'd frozen like that too. Then she'd woken up and frantically written down what she'd witnessed so that she wouldn't forget it.

"Ann-Marie, what did you see?"

"It didn't make any sense. But it seemed so real, like I was there."

"Quick. Tell me! Before it disappears!"

"It was this year's New Year's Eve dance. But that's impossible. It hasn't even happened yet. That's like being able to see…"

Marcus sighed. "The future."

Chapter 16

"Ann-Marie, you can't pretend nothing happened!" Marcus said, following his sister to her room. He was so used to hiding the magical part of his life, denying that it even existed, that he was tempted to act as if the whole vision thing hadn't happened too. But he couldn't. Because he needed to know everything about what his sister had seen. It could be important.

"Leave me alone." She tried to slam the door in his face, but he blocked it with his foot.

"Come on, talk to me. You saw the future, okay? I know it sounds crazy, but—"

"Crazy? Crazy doesn't even begin to cover it. I just zoned out for a second. Probably had too much sugar or something. It wasn't a vision or whatever you called it. It was nothing."

"Please, Ann-Marie. At least tell me what you saw! You said it was the New Year's Eve dance? What was happening? What did you see?"

"Nothing," she said.

"Was I there? Was Lena? Anyone you knew?"

She shrugged. "What difference does it make?"

He struggled to remember what he knew about how the visions worked for Natalie. He remembered her scribbling things down in her notebook, not just what she'd seen but phrases that stuck with her. Things like "Alice ruined by red" which, it had later turned out, had been about Lena crash-landing onto the stage during the school's production of *Alice in Wonderland*.

"Okay, if you didn't see anything, were there any words you remember? Any phrases? Anything?"

"Will you leave me alone? I have homework to do!"

"It's vacation!" Marcus roared. "Can't you take a break for five seconds and *talk* to me?"

His sister blinked at him. He realized he'd never screamed at her like this before. He'd never had the guts.

"No kiss at midnight," she said finally.

"What?"

"It's stupid, but those words were in my head when I, you know, woke up. Are you happy?"

"But what does that mean? What else—"

"That's all I know," she said. "Now leave me alone!" Then she shoved him out of the way and slammed the door in his face.

When Lena got back to her mom's apartment, she was drenched with sweat. She'd never pedaled so fast in her life. When she didn't see her mom's car parked in its usual spot, she thought she was safe. She could slip into the apartment before Mrs. Martinez woke up, stash the bike back where she'd found it, throw away the note she'd left, and pretend that she'd been working on memorizing her lines the entire time her mom was gone.

Then Lena went around the building and saw her mom's car out front, as if her mom had parked it in a rush. As if she's been determined to get home before Lena did. Uh-oh. Then Lena checked her phone. Eleven missed calls, all from her mom. Oh no. She'd been so intent on getting back as fast as possible that she hadn't even noticed it ringing.

When Lena pushed her bike through the apartment door, she found her mom on the phone with the police. There was no sign of Mrs. Martinez.

Her mom gave Lena a hard look and then explained to the police that her "missing daughter" had returned. She hung up the phone and sat stiffly on the edge of the couch. Lena didn't dare move.

The room throbbed with silence. Should Lena apologize before her mom started yelling at her? Would that make things better?

"Where's the milk?" her mom finally asked.

Lena blinked. "Milk?"

Her mom held up the note Lena had left on the table. "It says you went to get some milk." She crumpled the note in her fingers. "Mrs. Martinez told me that she came out of the bathroom and didn't know where you were. She called me in a panic. I was already on my way back, so I rushed here to find you gone and my bike missing. So where's the milk?"

"There was no milk," Lena admitted, leaning the bike against the wall. "That was a lie. But Mrs. Martinez lied too. She was asleep when I left!"

Lena's mom raised an eyebrow. Clearly, blaming Mrs. Martinez wasn't helping.

"I'm sorry," Lena went on. "I just…" But what could she say? If her mom was this mad about her going to get milk, she'd lock her in the closet if she found out Lena had her soul-hunting powers. "I had to get out of here, that's all," Lena added, and that felt like part of the truth, at least. "At home, I can be by myself anytime. But ever since I got here, I haven't had a second alone except when I'm in the bathroom. I had to go do something by myself for once." She took a step toward her mom. "You can understand that, can't you?"

Her mom's mouth tightened. "Do you really expect me to accept the fact that you've disappeared and that I don't know where you are? That you lied about where you were going? That you weren't answering your phone?"

"I wouldn't have to lie if you just trusted that I could take care of myself. Dad doesn't worry about me crossing the street by myself!"

"Well, I'm not your father, and I can't help worrying. That's what moms do."

Lena couldn't believe what she was hearing. "What about all those years you were gone? You only saw me at Christmas. You had no idea what I was doing the rest of the time."

Her mom gave her a wide-eyed, hurt look that made Lena's stomach churn. "Trust me," she said, her voice tight. "I thought about you constantly. I was always wondering how you were feeling, what you were up to."

"Funny how you never called to check on me," Lena said. "No emails, no texts from you. Nothing. I didn't even know what state you were in half the time!"

Her mom drew in a sharp breath, and Lena realized how angry her own voice had sounded. Apparently, she was a lot more upset about her mom leaving than she'd wanted to admit.

"Lena, I can't change the past, but now that we're here together, I expect to have some ground rules."

"Ground rules?" Lena repeated. "Are you kidding?"

"You can't just wander around by yourself—"

"Why not?" Lena cried. "I've been doing it for years without your help. So can you please stop treating me like I'm still a little kid?"

"That's not what I'm doing," her mom said. "I'm simply—"

"I can't even eat a sandwich without you getting involved!" Lena cried. "You can't leave me for three years and then show up and start acting like my mom again."

"But I *am* your mom. What do you expect me to do?"

Lena was saved from answering by the sound of her phone ringing. It was Marcus.

"I should take this," Lena said.

"But we're not done talking."

The phone quieted, but an instant later, Marcus sent her a message: SOS!

"Sorry. It's important," Lena said. Then she hurried to her room, glad to have an excuse to end the conversation. She'd already said things she knew she'd regret. She couldn't let anything else slip out.

"Lena, I think my sister somehow got Natalie's powers!" Marcus said when he answered the phone. Then he launched into an explanation of what had happened. "She saw a vision of the New Year's Eve dance and said something about 'no kiss at midnight.' What do you think it means?"

Lena's head was pounding. "I don't know, Marcus." She

couldn't believe her mom had called the police! Did she really think Lena was so helpless?

"She must have had the vision for a reason," Marcus said. "We need to figure it out. Maybe it's the key to fixing this power outage somehow!"

"Okay, let's start over." Lena tried to focus, but her brain was ready to burst. "You said that your sister got Natalie's powers?"

"Are you okay?" Marcus asked. "You sound weird."

"My mom and I kind of had a fight, but…" Lena shook her head. "I don't really want to talk about it."

"Are you sure? It might help."

Lena sighed, remembering what Hayleigh had said about her giving people the cold shoulder. Maybe she did shut people out sometimes. It was usually easier that way. But this was Marcus. She could open up to him without worrying about things going wrong.

"My mom…she's trying to be really strict all of a sudden, which is ridiculous, since she's been checked out of my life for years. I can't even tell her about my new powers or anything because—"

"Wait, she still doesn't know? Lena, you have to tell her. We both know that having someone else's powers could be dangerous!"

"Ugh, Marcus. You sound just like her."

"Well, maybe she's right. Maybe you should—"

"Just forget it, okay?" So much for trying to be open with people.

"But you can't—"

"Look, Marcus. I know you're trying to help, but I already have to listen to my mom tell me what to do all the time. I really don't need advice from someone who has to text me to figure out what color socks to wear!"

There was a long silence, and Lena instantly felt bad. She wasn't mad at Marcus, not at all. It was just too much at once. But before she could apologize, Marcus said softly, "I know I've been texting you too much and stuff, but…"

"No, it's not that! I like hearing from you. But you were the one who said we'd figure out how to make things work if I came out here with my mom. Right now, you're acting like I'm still there."

"I just miss you, that's all," Marcus said. "I hate not seeing you and the scheduled phone calls and—"

"I miss you too! Things would be so much better if you were here with me. But…" She let out a breath. "Maybe the space is good for you. For both of us. It'll make us be our own separate people, you know?"

There was another long silence.

"Marcus?"

"I, um, I have to go."

"But what about your sister's vision? You said it could be important."

"Maybe you're right. It's time I started figuring stuff out on my own." Then he was gone.

Chapter 17

The last place Marcus wanted to be was the Y, a.k.a. the location of the New Year's Eve dance he *wouldn't* be attending, but Connie had insisted he come check out her plan for choosing Ann-Marie's perfect guy. Marcus wanted to make sure she didn't do anything crazy—again.

"There you are!" Connie said, hurrying over to him. "The other guys are already making signs for the dance. Come see."

"The other guys?" Marcus asked. He spotted Peter and Albert in the corner, hunched over huge pieces of poster board. "How did you get them to help?"

Connie smiled mysteriously. "I have my ways."

He expected Albert to be shooting death glares at Peter because of the whole Ann-Marie situation, but the two guys seemed to be happily working side by side, sharing a bucket of blue poster paint. Marcus was surprised to see that Albert was wearing another sweater that Connie had given him and that he'd styled his hair again—without the glitter this time.

Albert was still mostly his dorky self, but he looked a tiny bit more confident.

"So this is your plan?" Marcus whispered to Connie. "Make them both do manual labor for you?" He frowned. "Wait. Why are they making 'Get plenty of exercise in the New Year' signs?"

"Because *exercise* is one of the most misspelled words in the English language," Connie answered, as if that explained everything. Then she called out to Peter and Albert, "Okay, new assignment. Make a poster that has the words *felicitations* and *thorough* on it. And remember, no cheating and looking up words on your phones!"

"What kind of weird New Year's dance is this supposed to be?" Peter grumbled, but he started scrawling letters across a new piece of poster board. Albert got to work without a word, clearly too intent on perfectly spacing out his letters to make a fuss about what he was writing.

"You're giving them a spelling test?" Marcus hissed.

Connie shrugged. "You know what a turnoff bad spelling is? I'm doing your sister a favor."

"So if one of them is a better speller than the other, that's who you think she should be matched with?"

"Of course not," Connie said. "That's only the first test. There are two more. And if need be, we'll have a tiebreaker at the end. Now, can you help me blow up some balloons?"

"Connie, this is—"

"Brilliant?" she said, grinning. "Hey, I can always give them a little zap if you don't want to go to all this trouble."

That shut Marcus up for a second. "Fine," he said. "But I seriously doubt this is going to work." Then he sighed and started inflating balloons to hang up around the hall.

After the posters were finished, Connie went over to inspect them.

"Uh-oh, Peter! Points off for misspelling *thorough*! And Albert, I thought you were supposed to be smart. How could you get *honor* wrong?"

"I used the British spelling," Albert said. "It's more common throughout the world."

Connie clearly wasn't impressed with either guy's handiwork. "Okay, next up, let's have you do some balloon arrangements."

"Don't you have any heavy lifting we can do?" Peter asked. "Creative stuff isn't really my thing."

Meanwhile, Albert looked perplexed. "How do you arrange balloons? By color? Or shape? Or buoyancy?"

"Any way you want! Now get to it!" Connie said with a big wink in Marcus's direction. Apparently, this was another one of her tests, although Marcus wasn't sure what she was looking for. Why would Ann-Marie care about a guy's balloon-decorating skills?

"How did she convince you guys to help out?" Marcus couldn't help asking.

"Gym credit," Albert said as Peter simultaneously answered, "Community service."

Marcus wanted to laugh. He was willing to bet neither of the guys would get any type of credit for doing this. He had to hand it to Connie though. She was certainly resourceful.

When they were finished, Marcus had a small clump of silver balloons, Peter had a giant arrangement of every color balloon in the rainbow, and Albert had carefully selected balloons that were all identical in shape and size and buoyancy, each representing one of the primary colors.

Connie gave all three arrangements critical glances. "Peter, yours looks like a balloon factory threw that up, and Albert, yours is so boring, and Marcus—" She sighed. "Forget it. Clearly, a guy having an eye for style is too much to ask. Peter, I need your help with something else. Come over to the disco ball."

Peter sighed heavily but followed her to the middle of what was going to be the dance floor.

"Okay, now dance with me," Connie said, turning up a slow song on her phone.

"Seriously?" he asked.

"I need to see if the disco ball is the right height." She

pointed at the ceiling. "You're pretty tall. I want to make sure you won't hit your head."

Marcus watched, amused, as Connie insisted on slow dancing with Peter. He could practically see the checklist in her head. *Sweaty palms? Bad breath? Slumped posture?*

"Um, she won't make me do that too, will she?" Albert whispered.

"She might," Marcus said. "Sorry."

Albert let out a long sigh. "I guess if Ann-Marie and I are going to the dance together, I should get some practice."

"So she said yes?" Marcus asked.

"N-no…not yet. But she might, right? I was going to call her tonight to see if she'd made up her mind. Do you think that's a good idea?"

Marcus swallowed. "It can't hurt," he said, hoping he was right. The truth was, he liked Albert, and not just because he reminded him a lot of himself. He was a nice guy who just wanted someone to like him. It felt wrong to mess with his emotions the way Connie was doing.

At that moment, Connie stepped away from Peter, clearly fed up with his dancing skills. "Albert, you're up next!" she yelled across the hall.

Before Albert could obey (or pass out), Ann-Marie appeared in the doorway.

"Oh, you're here!" Connie cried, rushing over to her.

"Are you sure I can get extra math credit for being here?" Ann-Marie asked, a skeptical look on her face.

"Totally," Connie said. She turned to Marcus and the other guys and said, "How about you put up some streamers?" Then she looped her arm through Ann-Marie's and said, "Come see the signs Peter and Albert made. How do you feel about British spellings of words?"

Ann-Marie looked thoroughly bewildered as Connie led her around from the posters to the balloon arrangements. Then she started talking about Peter's two left feet. "I haven't danced with Albert yet though," Connie said in a loud whisper that echoed throughout the empty hall. "But I'm willing to bet he's not much better. Do you care if he's coordinated? I guess you would if you're thinking of going to the dance with him."

"Wait," Peter said, looking up from the roll of masking tape he was wrestling with. "Albert, you're going to the dance with Ann-Marie?"

"Oh, um." Albert shrugged. "It's not official or anything. I asked her, but..." He didn't seem to know how to finish that sentence.

"He's still waiting on an answer," Marcus explained.

Peter frowned as he spun the roll of masking tape on his

finger. Then he tossed it aside, got to his feet, and went over to Ann-Marie. "Can I talk to you for a second?" he asked.

Ann-Marie nodded while Connie scuttled away, looking ridiculously pleased with herself. Marcus was straining so hard to hear Peter's words that he was barely breathing.

"So there's a dance here in a couple of days," Peter was saying. "I was going to ask you, but I didn't think it would be your kind of thing. But I heard you might be going with Albert."

"I don't know." Ann-Marie tugged on her ponytail. "I hadn't really decided."

"Well, if you want to go with me, I think we'd have fun."

Marcus held his breath, and beside him, he could see Albert doing the same. He expected Ann-Marie to jump at the chance, but she hesitated. "I, um, I should probably study that night. But...maybe... Can I let you know later?"

"Oh, sure," Peter said, sounding disappointed. "Whenever. I guess I'll go hang up some more streamers." And then he shuffled away, looking a lot less confident than usual.

As Ann-Marie started working on decorating the tables, he could see the frown lines on her forehead. Meanwhile, Peter and Albert were no longer chummily working side by side. Instead, they were glaring at each other as they seemed to be competing over who could make better paper snow-flakes. And the whole time, Connie was happily whistling away, bouncing around the hall as if everything were going according to plan.

That's when Marcus realized that this had been Connie's strategy all along. Give Ann-Marie a way to compare the two guys—based on Connie's weird criteria—and then make them both ask her to the dance. And then watch the drama unfold.

>>— Chapter 18 →

O kay, here we are," Lena's mom said, parking in front of the theater before class. She turned off the car and unbuckled her seat belt.

"What are you doing?" Lena asked. "You don't have to walk me inside." If her mom saw any hint of Pearl's soul, there was no way she'd simply ignore it.

"I'll just walk you to the door," her mom said. "Then I'll know you got in safely."

Lena sighed. "Do you want to put handcuffs on me first?" Her mom had been watching her like crazy since the previous night. She'd even made Lena keep the bathroom door open when she showered, as if Lena would try to jump out the tiny window or something.

Her mom only gave her an unamused look and opened the car door. Lena was all nerves as they went toward the theater entrance, but her mom kept her word and didn't go inside.

"I'll see you at exactly 1:00 p.m.," her mom said.

"What about your assignments for today?" Yvonne had called that morning with two more.

Her mom shook her head. "You're my priority, okay? I'll be here." Then she reached out and looked ready to give Lena a hug, but Lena quickly jumped back. She couldn't risk it when her new powers kept flaring up on their own.

But when her mom frowned, Lena realized she'd taken her not wanting to hug her personally.

"Mom," Lena said, trying to smooth things over. "All that stuff I said last night, I—"

But she didn't have a chance to apologize, because at that moment, Miss Fine opened the front door.

"Good morning!" she called. "Lena, this must be your mother. You two look so much alike! It's nice to finally meet you in person." She gave Lena's mom a quick handshake. "Will you be able to come to the show on Thursday?"

Lena noticed a strange look pass over her mom's face as she pulled her hand away. But then her mom said, "Of course. I can't wait to see my little girl up onstage."

Suddenly, an alarm started going off somewhere in the building. Miss Fine's face tightened. "Excuse me. It seems someone opened the emergency exit. Again." She let out a frustrated laugh. "Maybe this time, I'll catch them in the act!"

As Miss Fine hurried away, Lena's mom stared after her, her lips pulled into a tight line.

"Mom? Is everything okay?"

"Have you noticed anything strange about your teacher?" her mom asked.

"Strange? Um, not really. I mean, she's pretty strict, but that's actually been kind of nice. Even if not everyone appreciates it. Why?"

Her mom shook her head. "It's nothing, only... You probably wouldn't notice this, because your powers haven't gotten stronger yet, but when I shook her hand, I saw a flash of her aura."

"Her aura? What about her aura?" Lena had started seeing faint auras after she and Marcus had swapped powers, but she hadn't really paid much attention to them. What did she care if someone was supposed to get a love boost or not?

"There was a haze around her," her mom said. "One that usually means a person is haunted."

"Haunted?" Lena repeated.

"Yes," her mom said. "By a wandering soul."

Instead of heading to class, the first thing Lena did was pop into the bathroom.

"Pearl?" she called out. "Pearl, are you around?" There was no answer, but Lena wasn't about to give up just yet. "Pearl, I know what your job is. It's to follow Miss Fine around, right? You're haunting her."

Still no answer.

"I won't let you hurt her," Lena went on. "So you better leave her alone from now on, okay? Or else…" She wasn't sure how to finish that threat. How could she protect Miss Fine from a soul she couldn't even find?

"I won't leave her alone," a voice said from behind her. Pearl's voice.

Lena whirled around to find the clump of light hovering in front of one of the bathroom stalls. It looked so much brighter than the first time Lena had seen it. Whatever energy boost Lena had accidentally given Pearl was clearly still going strong.

"Why not? What did she do to you?"

"Do to me?" Pearl asked, sounding surprised. "Nothing."

"Then why are you stalking her? I thought you were tied to this theater, but it's her you're tied to, isn't it? That's why only the shows she's done here have been canceled and postponed."

"Why are you accusing me of things?" Pearl demanded. "You said you wanted to help me."

"I am trying to help you! I need you to let go of Miss Fine, of whatever you think your job is, and move on to the After."

But Pearl didn't answer. This wasn't working. Lena took a deep breath and asked in a softer voice, "Don't you want to see Myrna again? I bet she's waiting there for you."

"You really think she is?" Pearl asked, sounding younger than she had a minute earlier.

"I do. You said the two of you used to sing when you were scared? Think of all the songs you can sing with her in the After." Lena tightened her hands at her sides, ready to call up her energy at any second. "You won't have to be scared little girls anymore."

"Girls? What girls?" Her voice was suddenly harsh again.

"You...you and Myrna," Lena stammered. "You'll be reunited and—"

"No," Pearl said. "No, I have a job here. You can't make me forget about that!" The air sparked with static electricity.

"Okay, okay," Lena said as the hair on her arms stood on end. "Calm down."

But it was too late. As Pearl started zipping around the bathroom again, Lena knew she'd blown her chance.

"You don't understand," Pearl was saying, moving so fast that she was a glowing blur. "No one understands."

"Then explain it to me!" Lena cried, but Pearl only rushed into the floor drain and was gone.

Chapter 19

As Marcus biked through his neighborhood, trying to shake the urge to call Lena, he braced himself for the dreaded ride past Caspar Brown's house. But this time, as Marcus sped by, he sucked in a breath and slammed on the brakes.

There sat Caspar Brown, the biggest bully in school, by the pond across the street from his house, having a picnic with a girl. It didn't seem to matter that it was freezing out. These two were curled up on a blanket laughing and feeding each other fruit. Love sparks were buzzing around them like flies.

Clearly, Connie had been busy.

Marcus inched forward, trying to see the girl's face. Suddenly, Caspar's eyes snapped up, and he caught Marcus staring. "What do you want?" he barked, back to his usual self.

"Um, nothing."

The girl turned around, and Marcus nearly cried out in surprise. It was Hayleigh! Why on earth was she having a romantic picnic with *Caspar*?

"Oh, hey, Marcus!" Hayleigh said. "Want to come have lunch with us?"

Caspar didn't look too thrilled about the idea, but he didn't object either.

"Aren't you guys a little cold?" Marcus asked.

Hayleigh giggled. "You don't even notice when you're having so much fun!" Then she grabbed Caspar's hand, and—to Marcus's shock—the guy grinned back at her.

"So...you guys are..." He couldn't even make himself ask the question. "When did..."

"It was the funniest thing," Hayleigh chimed in. "Connie and I were walking back from your house yesterday, and Caspar was outside throwing stuff into the pond, and we started talking and then—boom! It was like we suddenly noticed each other. Didn't we, snookums?"

Caspar grinned. Actually grinned! "Yup," he said. "I always thought she was sparkly on the outside, but now I see she's sparkly on the inside too."

Marcus just about fell over. Caspar Brown, the guy who'd once thrown Marcus into a Dumpster, had just used the word "sparkly"? There was no way this match could last! What was Connie thinking, zapping them?

"We're going shopping soon," Hayleigh said. "You want to come?"

"Shopping?" Marcus echoed.

Hayleigh gave Caspar an affectionate poke on the shoulder. "*Someone* is taking me to the New Year's Eve dance, but he doesn't have anything to wear!"

Caspar shrugged. "I've never been to a dance before. No one's ever wanted to go with me." He gave Hayleigh a shy smile.

And for a crazy moment, despite all the terrible things Caspar had done, Marcus found himself wanting these two to work out. Maybe all that stuff teachers spouted about bullies only lashing out at people because they felt bad about themselves was true. Maybe all Caspar needed was for someone to give him a chance.

"Why are you still here?" Caspar grunted at Marcus.

Or maybe he was still kind of a jerk.

"When Lena gets back, we should double-date!" Hayleigh said. "Wouldn't that be so much fun?"

Marcus coughed. "Um, yeah. Sure." Of course, by the time Lena got home, the sparks between these two would have already faded. There was no way they were meant to be a real match! But let them have fun while it lasted. The longer Caspar was mooning over Hayleigh, the less time he'd spend making Marcus's life miserable.

When Marcus got home, the house was oddly quiet. His

sister had pretty much been locked away in her room since her vision the night before. He was desperate to find out more about what she'd seen, but she refused to even look at him.

He expected his dad to be yelling and cursing in the bathroom, but there was only some soft humming. Humming? His dad never hummed.

Marcus cautiously peered into the bathroom and found his dad busily grouting the tile above the bathtub.

"Marcus, I didn't hear you come in. Any chance you could give me a hand?"

Whoa. Since when did his dad ask for help instead of demanding it?

"Um, sure," Marcus said. He approached carefully, waiting for his dad to bark at him for stepping on the tile wrong or something. But his dad only handed him another trowel and asked him to start on the other side.

"Where's Mom?" Marcus asked after a second. Lately, his mom had taken to playing loud music to help drown out the sound of his dad's hammering, but the house was silent.

"My mom?" his dad asked, furrowing his brow. "I assume she's at her house. Why do you want to know?"

Marcus laughed. He was definitely not asking about his

dad's mother. Honestly, he was a little bit scared of his dad's parents. "No, I mean Mom. *My* mom."

His dad shrugged and went back to scraping off a layer of grout. "I have no idea."

At that moment, the front door opened, and Marcus heard another foreign sound: laughter. It was his mom, and it sounded as though she were talking on the phone with one of her friends. "I just got home. I'll call you later, okay?"

"Who's that?" his dad asked, glancing up from his work.

"What do you mean?" Marcus asked.

"I mean, who's here?"

Ugh. Were things really so bad between Marcus's parents that his dad was going to pretend he didn't even know the sound of his own wife's voice?

His mom came down the hall and poked her head in. "Hi, Marcus. Wow, look at it in here."

Marcus's dad smiled—actually smiled. "It's coming along." Then he glanced back at Marcus and asked, "Are you going to introduce me to your friend?"

Huh?

"I'm Claudia," his mom said, holding out her hand. She had a pleasant smile spread across her face, the kind you'd give a total stranger.

A sinking feeling spread through Marcus's stomach.

"Bruce," his dad answered, jumping to his feet. Then he laughed as he held up his grout-covered hand. "I'd shake your hand, but—"

"Oh, no problem," his mom said. "It's nice to meet you."

That's when Marcus noticed something odd about his parents' auras. The normally boring, beige clouds around them were now darker and hazier, but there was something else: sparks. Love sparks. And there was something wrong with them. Usually, when couples were zapped, their love sparks bounced in between them, connecting them. But here, the sparks were separate, not connected at all. As if someone had tried zapping his parents but had failed. As if the zap had not only failed but backfired.

And suddenly Marcus realized there was only one person who could have done that. Connie "I'm a Natural Matchmaker" Reynolds.

Chapter 20

Okay, here we are," Lena's mom said as they pulled up in front of a tiny boarded-up grocery store. "Now stay in the car."

Lena glanced out the window at the deserted parking lot. "Can't I go with—"

"No," her mom said. "Lena, we talked about this. You are staying here and waiting for me while I take care of this soul, and you are not moving, no matter what."

"But what if—"

"Enough!" her mom said. "If I had my way, you'd be at home, but since you scared poor Mrs. Martinez half to death with your disappearing act yesterday, I have no one to watch you."

Lena was about to shoot back that she didn't need watching, but she held her tongue. If her mom would rather bring her along on an assignment than leave her home alone, at least that gave Lena a chance to be closer to the action. Even if she was going to be locked inside a car the entire time.

"Now stay," her mom said, getting out of the car.

"Woof," Lena couldn't help answering, feeling like her German shepherd, Professor, probably did whenever he got left behind somewhere. Lena promised herself she'd give him some extra belly rubs when she got back home.

As she watched her mom disappear around the side of the grocery store, Lena's phone beeped. She was surprised to see it was Marcus. She hadn't heard from him since their (kind of) fight the previous day.

Connie zapped my parents and it backfired so now they don't remember each other. Just thought you'd want to know.

Lena gasped. She read the message over again, sure she'd misread it. But no, it was all true. She would have expected Marcus to end the message with a plea for help, but that was it.

She tried to think of something to say. Finally, she wrote back: Your parents will be okay. Don't worry. Are you all right? Do you need help?

He didn't reply, which only made Lena feel more helpless. What *could* she do from thousands of miles away? Still, she hated the idea of Marcus having to deal with this on his own.

A minute later, Lena noticed movement outside of the grocery store. A faint glow was coming toward her. The wandering soul. She expected her mom to be right behind it, but there was no sign of her.

Holding her breath, Lena watched as the soul meandered over to the now-empty shopping cart area. It moved slowly away, almost as if it were pushing an invisible cart as it crossed the parking lot. Then it headed toward the car where Lena was sitting.

As it moved closer, Lena waited for it to change course or for her mom to emerge from the building, but neither happened. Instead, the soul inched toward the car until it was in front of the hood. Then it moved around to the side, toward the passenger door where Lena was sitting and trying not to move.

Where was her mom? What was the soul doing here?

At the door, the soul stopped. Lena heard knocking on the glass. "Miss?" a faint man's voice asked. "Do you need help with your groceries? Want me to put your cart away?"

Lena swallowed. Her mom would kill her if she did anything.

"Miss?" the voice came again. "Do you know where everyone went? I've been wandering around this place, and there's no one here. I...I want to go home."

Without warning, Lena's hands flared to life with pale blue light. She didn't dare move, but the soul seemed drawn to the light like a moth. It floated through the glass and then—*boom!*—there was a flash, and the soul was gone.

Lena fell back in her seat, sighing in relief.

Then she saw her mom running toward her, and her relief vanished. Had her mom seen the whole thing?

"Lena!" her mom cried, throwing open the car door. "Are you okay? I told you to stay put!"

"I did! The soul came to me. It was asking if I needed help with my groceries."

"Then what happened?" Thankfully, her mom must not have seen everything.

"The soul came at me and then…" Lena swallowed, hating that she had to lie. "It just moved on by itself. I didn't do anything. It was ready to go, I guess."

Her mom sighed, clearly relieved. "We were lucky it crossed over on its own." Then she gave Lena an examining nurse look. "Are you sure you're all right? You look a little flushed."

"I'm fine, Mom. Really."

After a second, her mom nodded and got behind the wheel. But she didn't start the car. Instead, she stared out the window into the shadowy parking lot.

"Mom, are you okay?" Lena asked.

"I don't know if this is working," she said.

"The car? Maybe the battery's dead."

"No, this job." Her mom shook her head. "Me as a soul hunter. I thought it was what I wanted, but maybe I was wrong. And with the power outage and my having to put you in danger—"

"I'm not in danger!"

"Maybe…maybe it doesn't make sense for me to do it anymore."

Lena stared at her. "You mean you'd quit being a soul hunter?"

"Is it so wrong to want a normal life? Then I could finally fill my life with things that make me happy. I can't even remember the last time I had a second to work on a quilt."

"But you can't give up being a soul hunter!" Lena said. "This is part of who you are. Who *we* are."

Her mom gave her a long look, her face so tired that her eyes seemed sunken. "Maybe not anymore." Then she started the car and headed back home, as if the conversation were over.

As Lena replayed everything that had happened, everything her mom had said, she kept coming back to the same thing over and over. Her mom claimed she wanted to fill her life with things that made her happy, but until Lena had come back into her life, her mom *had* been happy. When she'd visited Lena before Christmas, she hadn't been able to stop talking about her great new life in Arizona. What if she quit soul hunting and was still miserable? What if her mom realized the reason she kept running, the reason she was never content, was Lena?

Chapter 21

"I don't know what you're complaining about, Marcus," Connie whispered. "Your parents look perfectly happy to me."

"Are you kidding?" Marcus whispered back as they peered through the half wall between the kitchen and living room. "They're acting like they just met!"

Marcus's mom hovered uncertainly by the armchair with an art book under her arm while Marcus's dad hurriedly folded up the blankets he'd used when he'd slept on the couch. (There had been an awkward moment the night before when both of Marcus's parents had headed for the same bedroom, convinced it was theirs and theirs alone.)

"Did you sleep well?" his mom asked.

"Oh, fine, yes," his dad answered. "I've never slept on this couch before, but it's pretty comfortable."

His mom let out a confused laugh. "Well, of course you haven't slept on it before. You just got here!"

"Erm." His dad clearly didn't want to contradict her, but

as far as he was concerned, this was his house, and she was a guest here. But instead of barking something about it, as Marcus would have expected, he simply smiled and said, "Where's Ann-Marie?"

"She said she was going to the gym."

"Oh, that's right." He thought for a second, as if trying to remember something. "How do you know her again?"

"She's my daughter."

"That can't be right," his dad said, frowning.

"And how do you know my son Marcus?" his mom asked.

"He's my son. Wait, did you just say…"

The two of them stared at each other in confusion for a second and then laughed and started talking about the weather, their conversation from a second ago completely forgotten thanks to the weird spell they were under.

"See? They're getting along," Connie said. "Way better than they were a couple of days ago."

Marcus shook his head. "So you really did zap them." He'd been hoping for some other explanation, but nothing else made sense. The only good thing about the situation was that the house had been a lot calmer. Ann-Marie had mostly locked herself in her room, clearly in "weird stuff overload," and Marcus's parents were being superpolite to each other, like houseguests who didn't want to wear out their welcome.

"Well, duh," Connie said. "Of course I zapped them. They were a mess! When I left your house the other day, they were arguing about mulch. I mean, really? *Mulch?* So I figured I'd do them a favor." She shrugged. "How was I supposed to know it would backfire?"

Marcus practically banged his forehead against the wall. "Because you didn't listen to me! I told you that going around zapping everyone would cause trouble. My parents were already matched. Matching them again made the sparks between them go crazy and made them forget each other!"

His parents were now sitting in polite silence, obviously too afraid to say anything to each other. Marcus couldn't stand to see them this way.

"Ugh, come on," he said, waving Connie down the hall to his room.

"I think you're missing the point," Connie said as she flopped into a chair in front of Marcus's worktable. "The fact that they don't remember each other is good news."

"How exactly is that good news?"

"Because there was still a spark between them!" Connie said. "Even though they were arguing all the time and stuff, they were still into each other. That means there's still hope that they won't split up like my parents did."

Marcus opened his mouth and shut it again. Maybe

Connie did have a point. Honestly, he'd been starting to doubt his parents had any sparks left between them at all. He certainly hadn't noticed any, but then again, his parents were just his parents. He'd never looked at their auras that closely before.

"But what if they never remember each other?" Marcus asked. "What if you wiped their memories of one another forever?"

Connie shrugged, picking up one of the robot models displayed above the table. "Then you just have to reintroduce them." Her face lit up. "In fact, I have an idea—"

"No!" Marcus cried, snatching the model away from her. "No more of your ideas! I'm done listening to what you have to say and following your crazy schemes and standing by and letting you match up everyone you want. I mean, Caspar and Hayleigh? Really? Are you crazy?"

Connie puffed out her cheeks. "If you don't want my help anymore then—"

"I never asked for your help! You just bulldozed your way into my life and started telling me—and everyone else—what to do. But I'm not going to let you do that anymore, not when it ends like this!"

"Fine!" Connie said, jumping to her feet. "Then you're on your own. And don't bother coming to the dance tomorrow, because you're not welcome anymore!" She started for the door and then slowed down, as if waiting for Marcus to stop her and apologize. But he only stood by, his arms in front of his chest, and waited for her to leave.

She huffed again and this time stormed out of his bedroom for real. Marcus stood in his doorway, watching her go. A second later, she slammed the front door behind her.

"Wow, everyone seems to be slamming doors these days," Marcus heard his dad say, obviously trying to hide his annoyance. "Between that and the smell coming from the basement..." He laughed. "Not to mention the torn-up bathroom. It's not exactly the best place to relax."

"Maybe we should go for a walk," he heard his mom say. "Get some fresh air."

A walk? Marcus couldn't remember the last time his parents had gone on a walk by themselves, let alone together. He crept down the hallway and watched as they left side by side, his dad holding the door open for his mom like a gentleman.

On their way out, they passed Ann-Marie, who was lugging her gym bag around, as usual.

"Ann-Marie, there you are," his mom said, stopping on the porch. "Have you met Bruce?"

Ann-Marie stared at her.

"Oh, Claudia," Marcus's dad said. "Have you met my daughter?"

Marcus expected his sister to roll her eyes and tell their parents to stop being freaks, but she only stood there, totally still.

"We're going for a walk. Be back in a little while," his dad said, giving Ann-Marie a little wave. Then their parents brushed past her and went down the walkway.

Marcus glanced back at his sister, whose face had gone stony. "No way," she said. "This is not happening." Then she stomped over to Marcus, her eyes full of venom. "What did you do?" she demanded, dropping her gym bag on the floor.

"What are you talking about? I didn't do anything!"

"First the weird dance thing and now this? Are you drugging me or something? Is that why I'm seeing things?"

"Wait. Did you know this was going to happen to Mom and Dad? Did you have another—"

"A *vision*?" she cried. "Of course not. That's insane. People don't see the future. They don't!" She kicked the corner of the couch, looking ready to tear it apart.

"Okay, calm down," he said firmly. "Tell me what happened." To his surprise, it worked.

"This morning," Ann-Marie said through her teeth, "I was in the shower, and all of a sudden, I was in another one of those dreams again. I saw Mom and Dad introducing themselves to each other like total strangers. I told myself it was nothing, but now I come home and find *this*." She shook her head. "What's happening to me, Marcus? What is this?"

"I…" How could he explain so that his sister would actually believe him?

"Please, Marcus," Ann-Marie said, and he was shocked to see tears in her eyes. "Help me."

Chapter 22

Lena didn't say a word to her mom the whole way to the theater. She was afraid that one more wrong word from her would make her mom quit being a soul hunter on the spot or go driving into the sunset again without a glance back at the people she was leaving behind.

When they got to the theater, Lena didn't even object when her mom walked her into the building. Anything to keep the peace for a little while longer.

But the instant they set foot inside the empty lobby, Lena spotted Pearl zipping past the chandelier. Oh no. Had her mom seen?

Thankfully, no. "I can't wait for the show tomorrow," her mom was saying. "I always hoped you'd get the acting bug from me. Who knows? Maybe once I have a little more free time, I'll go back to doing theater too. If I can work up the courage to get back onstage again, that is."

"Mom, are you sure about quitting soul hunting? Maybe you should—"

Just then, Pearl whizzed by again, and this time, Lena's powers clicked on like a lamp. A blue, blinding, potentially lethal lamp. Lena tried to shove her hands behind her back, but it was too late.

"Lena!" Her mom gasped, her gaze locked on Lena's glowing fingers. "What are you...how did you..."

"Watch out!" Lena called as Pearl came around for another pass. "Pearl, what are you doing? Leave us alone!"

Pearl's humming echoed through the lobby. "You're no fun," she said. "Myrna liked to play games with me. She was the only one who did."

Lena's hands were still glowing, but the light was fading now as Pearl went higher and higher. Then, after a second, she disappeared into the ceiling, and the lobby was empty again.

"Lena," her mom breathed beside her. "What just happened? Were your fingers..."

There was no point in hiding it now. No point in lying about this or about anything. As her energy faded and her hands went back to normal, Lena nodded and said, "Yeah, I guess I have your powers now."

"But-but how? Since when?"

"It's been a few days. They showed up the day after I got

here. Somehow you passed them on to me, I guess. Eddie said it's been happening all over the world."

Her mom shook her head, as if she couldn't believe what she was hearing. Then she glanced up at the gold-painted ceiling. "And the soul?"

"Her name's Pearl. She's the one who's haunting Miss Fine, although I can't figure out why. And instead of getting rid of her, your powers only made her stronger."

"Wait, you used my powers on her?"

"I tried, but I guess I did it wrong—"

"Of course you did it wrong! You haven't been trained!" Her mom grabbed at her temples as if she had a sudden headache. "I can't believe this. Why didn't you tell me? Why did you hide all this from me?"

"Because…" But how could she explain? *I didn't want you to get overwhelmed and run again?*

Her mom couldn't seem to stop shaking her head. "You had no right to keep this from me! They're my powers, and you've been using them. Do you have any idea how much danger you've put yourself in?"

"Me? I didn't do anything! They just came to me. And for your information, besides the Pearl thing, I've been doing just fine with your powers. How do you think the souls at the yoga place and at the grocery store moved on?"

Her mom's eyes went even wider. "That was you?"

"I didn't mean to. It just happened, but if it wasn't for me, those souls would probably still be wandering around. I helped you!"

"By lying to me?" her mom practically roared. "And hiding things from me? And running around God knows where, using my powers behind my back?" All of a sudden, she stopped moving, her body growing very still. "No. No. That's it. We're done."

"Done with what?"

"With everything!" her mom cried. "This class. Letting you out of my sight. It was all a mistake. I should have protected you more from the minute we got off that plane."

Lena couldn't believe it. "How could you have protected me more? By chaining me up? You've already made life here almost unbearable! If it wasn't for this class, I'd be going totally insane."

"Come on," her mom announced. "We're going home."

"Now? But we're doing one last run-through before the show tomorrow."

"We'll tell Miss Fine that you have to pull out of it."

Lena was so shocked, all she could do for a second was laugh. Then she managed to whisper, "Are you really going to punish me by taking me out of the show?"

"I'm not punishing you. I'm trying to protect you. I can't lose you again. Don't you understand that? I can't!"

"Lose me?" Lena asked in disbelief. "You're the one who left! You didn't lose me. I lost you!"

At that moment, Miss Fine came out of the employee entrance. "Is everything all right?" she asked. She must have heard them yelling.

"I'm sorry," her mom said, "but Lena is going to have to withdraw from the show."

Miss Fine stepped back in surprise. "But it's tomorrow."

"It's a family matter," her mom said. "I apologize for the timing, but—"

"No," Lena said. She was done letting her mom tell her what to do. "I'm performing in the show."

Her mom's jaw tightened. "Lena—"

"You can't do this, Mom. You're not protecting me. You're hurting me. And I won't let you do it anymore."

Miss Fine looked back and forth between them. "Obviously, you two have a lot to talk about—"

"There's nothing to talk about. I'm staying here," Lena announced. Then she walked past Miss Fine and into the theater. She didn't know if her mom was watching her walk away or if she'd marched out of the theater too, but Lena didn't let herself look back.

Chapter 23

Okay, spill it," Ann-Marie said, sinking down on Marcus's bed. "What's happening to me?"

Marcus leaned back in his desk chair. Where to start? "I'm a matchmaker," he said, deciding to just dive in. "Like Cupid but without the diaper. And Lena's a soul collector. Like a grim reaper but without the—"

His sister shot to her feet. "Forget it. If you're just going to tell me fairy tales, then—"

"Ann-Marie, I'm serious!" Marcus cried. "You don't have to know about our powers, I guess, but you have to understand that there's a whole web of them. There's a network of magical stuff happening all around us, and I'm part of it. And now, you're part of it too. That's what the visions are."

He expected her to throw open the door and stomp out, but she stood with her hand resting on the doorknob. "A network?"

"Yeah. Except the network's down. Or it's malfunctioning.

Which means that you got someone else's powers, and now you can see glimpses of the future."

She sighed, rubbing her chin. "Okay…so say that I believe you—and I'm not saying I do—does that mean I'm stuck with these weird visions now?"

"No, your powers should fade," Marcus said. "And eventually, Natalie will get them back. Or, at least, I hope she will."

"Natalie? The girl who was here the other day?"

"Yeah, you must have swapped powers when you crashed into her."

Ann-Marie let out a strange laugh. "What if I pushed her into a potted plant again? Would that make things go back to normal?"

Marcus chuckled. If only things were so easy. "This power outage thing is a lot bigger than just us. That's why Mom and Dad are acting so weird. It's because of my powers."

Ann-Marie's eyes widened. "You did this to them? Why? Because of you, they're acting like they've never met!"

"No! No way! I would never zap people who were already matched. But this girl got my powers, and even though I told her not to use them, she—" He could tell he was losing Ann-Marie again. "It doesn't matter how it happened. And honestly, I don't know how to undo it, but usually in this kind of situation, we just have to wait things out, and it'll all right itself."

"In this kind of situation?" Ann-Marie repeated. "You mean you've dealt with this kind of stuff before? And you were able to fix it?"

"Um, yeah. Sort of…" Had he actually fixed anything in the past? He and Lena had managed to get things back to normal together, but he couldn't take credit for that. In fact, if Lena hadn't been there pushing him along, he wondered if he would have simply sat by and waited for their past problems to go away.

"Then you can figure it out again. Can't you?" Ann-Marie asked. "Because I have enough going on right now. I can't deal with all of this…whatever it is."

Her voice was gruff as usual, but there was an odd pleading look in her eyes. It was clear that she wanted Marcus to tell her that he had the answer, that he knew a way to make everything all right again.

Marcus realized that this must have been how Grandpa Joe felt all those times Marcus had asked him for advice, for reassurance, for hope. Grandpa had always seemed so sure of himself, so certain that things would be okay. But maybe that had all been an act because he'd realized Marcus had needed to hear it.

"Marcus?" Ann-Marie said. "You can fix things, right?"

And even though Lena wasn't there to help him and he didn't have anything close to a plan, he nodded and said, "Absolutely."

"Thanks for meeting us," Marcus said, waving Natalie over to a seat in a deserted corner of the public library. "You remember my sister?"

"Sorry again about crashing into you," Ann-Marie said. "And about taking your powers or…or whatever the right thing is to say in this kind of situation."

Natalie shrugged. "At least I know my powers are still around. I was afraid I might have lost them forever." She turned to Marcus. "You said you needed my help?"

"We need to figure out how to undo this power outage."

Natalie laughed. "Don't you think everyone is already trying to do that?"

"Yeah, but they're looking at big stuff that caused it. I think it was something else, something small."

"Why do you say that?"

"Because it always is, isn't it? A chain reaction starts with something tiny and gets bigger and bigger." That's exactly what had happened with Connie. He'd let her get away with a few tiny matches, and now she'd practically zapped the entire town. Just on his way to the library, he'd passed half a dozen couples who were disgustingly gaga for each other.

"Okay, so what do we do?" Natalie asked.

"Your visions let you know about important stuff that's about to happen, right? Well, Ann-Marie's had two visions so far. Maybe you can help us figure out what they mean." He turned to his sister. "Go ahead and tell her what you saw."

Ann-Marie hesitated. "It wasn't just seeing stuff. It was like...all these hazy images and random thoughts floating around. It's hard to remember."

"You don't have to remember all of it," Natalie said. "I've kind of trained myself to focus on one main thing and then to write it down the minute I snap out of the vision. Try to think back to the major stuff. Sometimes even one word is enough to be helpful."

Ann-Marie nodded and closed her eyes. "Okay, so the first vision was...well, it was this year's New Year's dance at the Y."

"How could you tell it was this year's?" Marcus asked.

"Or that it was at our Y?" Natalie broke in. "Those places all kind of look the same."

"Because there were some of the weird misspelled posters Connie hung up everywhere," Ann-Marie said, her eyes still closed.

Marcus wanted to laugh. Maybe Connie's wacky spelling test had been more helpful than he'd realized.

"What else did you see?" Natalie asked.

"I…don't know." Ann-Marie's eyes flew open. "It's too hazy. I can't remember!"

"You said there was a phrase that was stuck in your head," Marcus jumped in. "Something like, 'No kiss at midnight.'"

"I did?" Ann-Marie shook her head. "I don't really remember."

"Did you see people kissing at the dance?" Marcus asked.

Ann-Marie thought for a second, her eyebrows furrowed. "No," she said finally. "Just everyone dancing and having fun."

"Was it midnight in your vision?" Natalie asked.

"I don't know," Ann-Marie answered. "There was a clock… and maybe it said midnight." She looked at Marcus. "I'm sorry. That's really all I remember."

"It's okay," Marcus said, but he couldn't help feeling disappointed. He'd hoped his sister would be able to give them something else to go on. "What about the second vision?"

"It's just what I already told you," Ann-Marie said. "Yesterday when I was at the gym, I saw a flash of Mom and Dad introducing themselves to each other like they'd never met before. They were standing in our bathroom at home."

Marcus nodded. "That's exactly what happened. But why would you see it as it was happening? What's the point? You couldn't stop it."

"Maybe she wasn't supposed to stop it," Natalie broke in. "Some of my visions just show me things that are happening.

I don't always know why. Maybe to reassure me that they're going the way they're supposed to."

"My parents losing their memories of each other is meant to happen?" Marcus asked. "Seriously?"

Natalie shrugged. "I'm just telling you how things work. But when I see something before it happens, sometimes it means I'm supposed to stop it from coming true."

"Sometimes?" Ann-Marie asked. "What about the other times?"

"That's when I'm supposed to try to help it come true."

"So if her vision was about 'no kiss at midnight'?" Marcus asked. "What does that mean?"

"Someone isn't supposed to kiss at midnight on New Year's Eve," Natalie said.

"Well, if it's me, that's easy. Connie pretty much banned me from going to the dance, and Lena won't be there anyway," Marcus said.

"And I have…" Ann-Marie laughed. "Well, I guess I kind of have two dates, but I'm not planning on kissing either of them!"

"Wait," Marcus said. "You said yes to both Albert and Peter?"

"Not exactly," Ann-Marie said, her cheeks turning pink. "But when I tried to turn them down, they both kind of assumed I'd meet them there."

Natalie chuckled. "Well, I definitely don't have that problem. I'm not even going to the dance."

"Okay, so maybe…" Marcus's brain swirled. He'd made such a big deal about the midnight kiss, how important it was to set the tone for the rest of the year. But maybe the opposite was true too. If you didn't kiss someone, you started the year with a clean slate, in a way. Maybe that was the key to fixing things. "We have to keep everyone at the dance from kissing at midnight."

Natalie stared at him. "Everyone?"

"If we don't know who it's supposed to be, we have to make sure no one does."

"But that's impossible! How are you going to do that? Shut down the dance?"

Marcus shook his head. He seriously doubted Connie would let him cancel the party she'd worked so hard to organize. But maybe… "Connie Reynolds is the queen of getting people to kiss at parties, right? Maybe she's the one we need to talk to."

Chapter 24

L ena, are you all right?" Miss Fine asked, sitting down next to her during the class break. "Your mom seemed pretty upset when she left."

"Yeah, sorry about all of that," Lena said, staring at her uneaten animal crackers. "I guess we have some, um, unresolved issues we're dealing with."

Miss Fine gave her an understanding smile. "It's tough when you and your mom don't see eye to eye. Before my mom passed, she and I argued a lot. She always saw the bright side of things, always told me to relax, to let things happen, but I..." She laughed. "I could never do that. I always liked being in control."

Lena nodded. She could certainly relate to that.

"But you know what?" Miss Fine said. "After a while, I realized that—"

Suddenly, a fire alarm sounded. Everyone jumped to their feet.

"Okay, stay calm!" Miss Fine called out. "I'm sure it's a false alarm. But let's go outside. Single file."

Lena could tell the other kids were nervous. All except Shontelle, who had a smug smile on her face. "I told you guys this place was haunted!" she said with some dramatic finger wiggling.

Zade and Luis both laughed, but Lena's stomach sank. What if that's exactly what was happening? What if Pearl was acting out again? She already liked to set off the alarm on the emergency exit. Why not step things up and hit the fire alarm instead?

When the group filed out through a back door, Lena hung back at the end of the line. Then, when no one was looking, she slipped off toward the piano in the lobby where Pearl liked to hang out.

"Pearl?" Lena called out. "Pearl, I know you're here! Why are you trying to drive everyone out?"

She crinkled her nose. There was a weird smell in the air. Not popcorn this time, but something else. Before she could place it, she spotted the clump of light coming toward her.

"You shouldn't be here," Pearl said.

Lena shook her head. "No, *you* shouldn't be here. You need to move on, Pearl. It's time to leave Miss Fine alone and *go*."

"Get out."

"You can't do this!" Lena went on. "You don't understand

how important this class is to me. How important this show is to me. I've been dreaming of being onstage for years. This is finally my chance, and I won't let you ruin it. I won't! Not after everything I've given up to be here!"

Lena took a step back. Wow, she hadn't realized how much this class really meant to her. Nothing like spilling your guts to a soul to make you realize how you felt.

But all Pearl said was, "Get out."

"Listen, Pearl. I'm trying to—"

"*Get out!*" Pearl shrieked, so loudly that the chandeliers rattled. Then the door behind Lena flew open, and she felt herself being shoved toward it.

"Stop it!" Lena said, struggling to free herself. "Don't you see that I'm trying to help you? The more you fight me, the harder it'll—"

But she was already outside. Before she could fight her way back into the theater, the door slammed shut, and Lena heard it lock with a loud click. Then she was alone in an alley by the side of the theater.

As fresh air filled her lungs, she realized what the odd smell inside the lobby had been. It was gas. There was a gas leak in the building.

She ran toward the front of the theater where the other kids were waiting on the sidewalk.

"Lena!" Zade cried. "Where did you go? Miss Fine went back in to look for you. She said to wait here until the fire department came."

Lena gasped. "Oh no! She needs to get out of there!"

She ran toward the door but it was locked. Gah! Lena tried a nearby window and another. Then she ran back to the door Pearl had pushed her through, but it still wouldn't budge.

No! This had to be what Pearl had been waiting for. After years of stalking Miss Fine, Pearl had finally decided to attack her. Well, Lena wasn't going to just stand by and let it happen!

She spotted a nearby window with a crack down the middle. Frantic, she grabbed a rock and flung it through the glass. She crawled in, managing to avoid the broken shards, and then ran through the theater, screaming Miss Fine's name. No answer.

When she got to the lobby, near the piano, she gasped. There was Miss Fine, sprawled out at the bottom of the staircase, unconscious. And she wasn't alone. Pearl was hovering over her, her light glowing brighter than ever.

"Get away from her, Pearl!" Lena cried, running over. "Get back!" Her hands flared to life without her even trying, and Pearl jumped away from the glow. Then she quickly fled through the ceiling.

After the energy had faded from her hands, Lena grabbed Miss Fine and started dragging her through the lobby. Her teacher was breathing, but there was blood trickling down her forehead as if she'd hit her head on something.

The gas smell was making Lena cough, but she kept pulling and pulling until finally—*crash!*—she burst through the front doors of the theater with Miss Fine in tow. She sucked in a breath of fresh air and lay Miss Fine on the sidewalk, cradling her head.

"Mom," Miss Fine whispered, squinting up at her. "Is that you?"

"N-no, Miss Fine. It's me. It's Lena. You're safe now."

Miss Fine smiled. "You were right, Mom, about the guardian angel. It saved me. I saw it. You were right." Then she closed her eyes and slipped into unconsciousness.

When the fire department came, everything was in chaos. Someone rushed Miss Fine into an ambulance, holding gauze to her forehead, while the firefighters inspected the building. Meanwhile, the world spun around Lena. Around and around like a carousel.

She vaguely heard the firefighters saying that workers must have hit a gas line when they were cleaning out the pigeon nests. She nodded when someone asked her if she was all right.

"No idea why the fire alarm went off," Luis said. "A gas leak wouldn't have triggered it."

"It must have been the ghosts," Shontelle answered. "They kept us out so we wouldn't get blown up."

"Yeah, right," Zade answered. "As if ghosts care about that kind of stuff."

All Lena could do was listen and try to stop her body from shaking. She'd thought Pearl had been trying to hurt Miss Fine. But maybe Lena had been wrong. Maybe Pearl had only been trying to help all along.

The drive to the hospital was pretty much silent. When Lena's mom had picked her up from the theater, she'd asked some general questions about what had happened. Lena had told her about the gas leak and about Miss Fine being injured, but she'd left out the part about Pearl. She didn't want to remind her mom about the soul or about her powers or about the fight they'd had that morning.

"I knew letting you out of my sight was a mistake," her mom said, her voice weary. Thankfully, she left it at that. Maybe she didn't want to rehash the fight either.

When they got to the hospital, her mom used her ID badge to park in the employee parking lot. They went into the building, and her mom stopped to chat with one of her nurse friends while Lena went down the hall to Miss

Fine's room. For once, it seemed, her mom was giving her a little space.

Miss Fine looked pale, and there was a bandage on her head, but otherwise, she seemed all right.

"Lena!" Miss Fine said. "I hear I have you to thank for helping to get me out of the theater."

Lena shrugged. "It's also my fault you were in that building in the first place. I'm sorry. I shouldn't have wandered away like that when the fire alarm went off. Are you okay?"

"A bit embarrassed, honestly. I can't believe I tripped on those darn stairs! I knew the carpet was loose, but I was rushing and not paying attention and..." She laughed. "Mostly, though, I'm annoyed that we didn't get to do a dress rehearsal."

"We're all going to practice on our own tonight," Lena said. "We'll be ready for tomorrow. Don't worry." She swallowed. "Miss Fine, before you passed out, you said something about a guardian angel? And about your mom being right?"

Miss Fine blinked in surprise. "I did?" She seemed to think that over for a moment. "It sounds silly, but everything always seemed to line up for my mom. She claimed she had a guardian angel looking out for her. She said some kind soul was keeping an eye on her and that one day, that angel would look out for me too. I thought it was all nonsense until...until today when I felt someone—*something*—trying to help me out of that building. Before you ran in and dragged me out, I could have sworn someone else was there with me."

"Miss Fine?" Lena asked softly. "Your mom's name, was it Myrna?"

"No, no," Miss Fine said, shaking her head. "It was Martha."

"Oh."

"Myrna, that was my grandmother's name."

Lena stopped breathing for a second. "Who…who was she?"

"Well, let's see. She was a nurse. Like your mother, in fact. Except this was years and years ago, back when tuberculosis was a big problem." Miss Fine leaned her head against her pillow. "Grandma Myrna worked with kids who were sick. People would bring their kids to Arizona because of the warm, dry air. That was the only cure for tuberculosis back then. My grandmother loved the kids she worked with. She'd play the piano for them and sing songs. They were like her own children. Many of them recovered, but some didn't. She took those losses pretty hard. Eventually, she met my grandfather and stopped working to have kids of her own. By the time I was born, her memory was failing her. She didn't remember much about who she was or where she was, but she'd talk about those sick kids a lot. She still remembered all their names. Jacob, William, Elizabeth, Pearl. She'd tell us about them over and over and about the songs they loved to sing."

"What was Pearl's favorite song?" Lena asked. "Do you remember?"

Miss Fine thought for a long time and then let out a soft laugh. "Actually, I do." She started to sing, a low, sad lullaby that made Lena's skin tingle. This was it. This was how she was going to get Pearl home.

Chapter 25

As Marcus got dressed for the New Year's Eve dance, he couldn't stop looking at his phone. He'd tried calling and texting Connie, begging for her help, but so far, she hadn't responded. His only hope was to go to the dance, figure out a way to get inside, and avoid letting anyone there kiss at midnight. No problem, right?

He desperately wanted to call Lena and beg for her advice, but she was probably getting ready for her show. Besides, he couldn't keep relying on her for everything. He had to figure this one out on his own. Instead, he sent Lena a message wishing her luck with the show and left it at that.

He smoothed his unruly hair one more time and then went out into the living room to find his parents in the kitchen, unwrapping packages of newly purchased pizza dough.

"Um, what's going on?" he asked.

"Oh, Marcus," his dad said. "Claudia here was telling me about the big exhibit she has coming up. Isn't that exciting?"

"Yeah…" Marcus said. "Mom, don't we have enough dough?"

She sighed. "I realized the pieces weren't working because they didn't have enough structural support, so I scrapped them all and am starting over."

"What? You spent *weeks* working on those dough blobs!"

"It's all right, honey. Bruce is going to help me."

Marcus looked at his dad in shock. "*You're* going to help make sculptures?"

"Sure!" his dad said. "I'm not much of an artist, but I know about building things. If we put our minds together, we'll figure it out."

"As long as you can stand the smell!" his mom said, laughing. "This stuff gets moldy pretty fast."

To Marcus's surprise, his dad smiled and said, "If it means spending more time with you, I can handle a little mold."

His mom beamed back at him, and for a second, Marcus saw sparks flare between them. His chest swelled with hope. He'd thought Natalie was wrong about Ann-Marie's vision showing her what was meant to happen. Why would his parents be destined to forget each other? But this was the happiest he'd seen them in…well, maybe in forever. He remembered what his mom had said about the two of them talking about art and even making art together when they'd first met. Somewhere along the way, they'd lost that, but maybe it wasn't gone. Not completely. Maybe it could be rebuilt again.

Just then, Ann-Marie breezed out of her bedroom. Marcus almost fell over when he saw she was wearing a dress. He didn't think he'd ever seen his sister in anything besides T-shirts and running shorts. Then he glanced down and smiled. She might have been wearing a dress, but she was also wearing her sneakers.

"What?" Ann-Marie said.

"Nothing. You look good."

"Thanks," she mumbled. "So do you."

"Are you ready?" he asked.

She nodded. "Let's go."

As they headed to their bikes, Marcus realized this was possibly the first time ever that he and his sister had gone somewhere together on purpose. Weirdly, part of him hoped that maybe it wouldn't be the last.

The inside of the Y looked incredible. Besides a few odd posters featuring questionably spelled words, the hall was sparkly and shimmery and perfect to ring in the New Year. Connie had really done a great job. And even though it was still early, the place was already hopping with people.

"I'm going to go find Connie," Marcus told his sister.

"Let me know when you need my help," Ann-Marie said. She glanced around. "I guess I should find my dates."

"Go easy on Albert, okay?" Marcus asked, but Ann-Marie had already disappeared into the crowd.

He spotted Natalie on the other side of the room. Even though she hadn't wanted to come to the dance since she claimed she didn't have any friends, she'd agreed to be there in case Marcus needed extra help. He was glad to see her chatting with Abigail and Ty and even laughing a little bit. He was surprised to realize that thanks to the whole power outage mess, he actually trusted her now. The lies she'd told in the past didn't seem to matter anymore. After all, he knew what it was like to desperately want people to like you.

A minute later, Connie charged over to him. "What are you doing here, Marcus? I thought I uninvited you."

"You did and…I'm sorry for freaking out at you. I'm still not thrilled that you zapped my parents, but maybe it's not so bad. They're actually getting along, laughing and stuff. It's been a long time since that happened."

Connie pursed her lips. "Well, if you're sorry, then I'm sorry too. Maybe I did overdo it a little bit."

Marcus gave her a suspicious look. It wasn't like Connie to back down from anything or to admit that she'd been wrong. "What happened?"

She looked down at her strappy shoes. "The lady at the nail salon, the one I accidentally zapped first? Well, it turns out the guy she was matched with already has a girlfriend. Oops. I went in for a manicure this morning, and she spent the entire time crying. I realized that...well, you were right about some people not being meant to be together. I guess it was just fun to imagine the possibilities, you know?"

Marcus did know. That's what he liked about being a matchmaker. "You'll know better next time."

She shrugged, her glossy lips turning down at the corners. "I don't think there's going to be a next time. My powers are gone."

"What? How do you know?"

"Because when I tried to zap a couple at the grocery last night, my hands didn't light up or anything. So I guess it's over."

Marcus let out a relieved sigh. That, at least, was some good news. But he couldn't help seeing how bummed Connie looked. "You really liked doing it, didn't you?"

She shrugged. "It was nice to be good at something, you know? I mean, look at them!" She pointed to Hayleigh and Caspar who were—impossibly—slow dancing under the disco ball. "They look so happy. Even if it doesn't last, at least I gave them that for a little while, right?"

"Yeah, you did," Marcus said, and he had to admit she was

right. Even if Caspar went back to his old ways after the spark with Hayleigh faded, at least it proved that there was a part of him that wasn't all bad. "Listen, Connie. I need your help."

"Is this about all that 'no kiss at midnight' stuff you've been sending me messages about?" she asked. "Because you are insane if you think I'm going to let you mess up this dance."

"But the balance of the universe is at stake!" he cried.

Connie only crossed her arms, clearly unmoved.

"Please, Connie. If anyone can figure out what to do, it's you. You're a natural at all this relationship stuff." He hated to admit it, but it was true. Despite the chaos she'd caused with all her zaps, Connie had done some good too.

That seemed to get through to her. "I am pretty awesome." She sighed. "Okay, fine. I'll help you. But if anyone has a bad time at this dance, I will never forgive you. Got it?"

Marcus shuddered. He knew she meant it. Anyone who had ever played Truth or Dare at Connie's house knew the threats of toilet licking and other mortifying torture were very real.

"Got it."

"Okay, so what's your plan?"

He scrambled to pull a list out of his pocket.

"*Ten ways to avoid getting people to kiss at midnight?*" Connie read. She laughed. "Oh boy. Lena is definitely rubbing off on you."

Marcus smiled, wishing Lena could be by his side to help him go through this list. But if he couldn't have her there to help him save the day, at least he could do his darndest to show her that he could do it on his own. "Let's hope so."

Chapter 26

Lena couldn't stop shaking with excitement before the show. It was really going to happen. She was going to be onstage. In front of an audience. In an actual scene!

"Are you ready to go?" her mom asked.

Lena nodded and followed her out to the car. They still weren't speaking much, so the ride went by in silence. But when they pulled up in front of the theater and her mom walked her to the door, Lena was so excited that she couldn't help saying, "You'll be there, right? At the show? It starts in an hour."

Her mom looked at her. "If you still want me there."

"What? Of course I do."

"I wasn't sure...after everything."

She sounded so hurt that Lena felt the last of her defenses crumbling. "Mom, I'm sorry. I didn't mean for—"

Her mom shook her head. "Let's not talk about this now, okay? You have a show to prepare for. Break a leg." Then she turned and hurried back to her car.

Lena watched her drive away, her body suddenly heavy. She'd been trying to apologize, and her mom had just shut her down! She almost wanted to laugh as she remembered what Hayleigh had said about the Lena cold shoulder. Maybe all that "like mother like daughter" stuff people said was true.

When she went into the theater, passing the now-boarded-up window she'd had to crawl through the day before, Lena spotted a ball of light perched on the piano in the lobby. "Pearl?"

Something was wrong. Pearl's light was glowing so brightly, it looked ready to burst into flames. And it was eerily still.

"Pearl, are you all right?" Lena asked, hurrying over.

"I couldn't help her," Pearl said in a strange, quiet voice. "She was hurt, and I couldn't... It's my fault she's gone."

"Who? What are you talking about?"

"Myrna's granddaughter," Pearl said, her voice still oddly hushed. "I tried to help her, but I wasn't strong enough. And now I can't find her. She's gone."

"No, she's okay," Lena insisted. "She was at the hospital, but she'll be back here in time for the show—"

"The hospital?" Pearl screeched. "No, Melissa can't go there! People don't come back from there. I didn't. My friends didn't."

"Pearl—"

"I swore I'd look out for Myrna the way she looked out for

me," Pearl went on. "All these years, I've been looking out for her and for her daughter and her granddaughter, but it's over! I've failed!"

"Pearl, she's fine!"

"Then where is she?" Pearl thundered, the lights flickering overhead. "Melissa? Where are you? Where are you?"

Suddenly, the light pushed off the piano and whizzed past Lena's head, nearly sending her flailing backward. Thankfully, she caught herself on the banister.

"Pearl!" Lena cried, watching her disappear into the theater. Lena's head was pounding. The show was going to start in an hour. She couldn't let Pearl ruin it!

As the other kids started to warm up, Lena pretended to run lines while she scanned every inch of the entire theater, but she couldn't find Pearl.

Finally, Miss Fine came in and called for everyone to gather around. She still had a bandage on her forehead, but otherwise, she seemed like her old self. Well, almost.

"Zade," she said. "I want you to have fun with your role today."

"Really? But I thought you said—"

"I was wrong. Acting is work, but you have to capture the joy in it too. If you're trying to control everything, you lose the spontaneity, the fun. And that's where the magic comes from.

Sometimes you have to believe in a little magic." She gave Lena a wink and then told everyone to get into costume.

Lena smiled, but as they did their physical and vocal exercises, she couldn't stop scanning the walls and ceiling. Still no Pearl.

Finally, with ten minutes before the show, Lena's phone beeped. It was a message from Marcus. Break a leg, it said. You'll be great.

As Lena read the words over and over, guilt flooded through her entire body. She'd barely talked to Marcus since their fight, and yet there he was, thousands of miles away, struggling to figure out how to put their powers back the way they should be, and he still remembered to wish her luck before her big stage debut.

She put her phone down, her chest tight. She couldn't believe how stupid she'd been. Marcus had always been there for her, no matter what. And the one time he really needed her—for their sake and for the sake of so many others—she'd told him to figure it out on his own. He'd needed her, and she wasn't there. And now it was too late.

"Places!" Miss Fine called. "Places, everyone!"

Lena tried to shake thoughts of Marcus from her mind. Then she hurried toward the stage.

When the show started, Lena hovered in the wings, watching the scenes going on onstage while still scanning the theater for any sign of Pearl. Where could she be?

During the first scene, Lena spotted her mom at the end of the front row. She was also scanning the theater, obviously keeping an eye out for Pearl too.

Scene after scene went by, and finally it was Zade and Lena's turn. Lena took in a long, long breath. This was it. She had to stop thinking about Pearl and Marcus and everyone else. She had to be Wendy now. She tried to use her body the way Miss Fine had taught her, putting herself in someone else's shoes for a little while. Then she and Zade took their places.

As the scene started, the first thing Zade did was peel an imaginary banana. Lena actually laughed in surprise. But not as herself, as Wendy. Who was this strange monkey boy? Wendy was delighted at the sight.

As the scene continued, Lena stopped thinking about everything else and just became Wendy. And for the first time, she wasn't calculating and planning and controlling every little thing Wendy did. She was just having fun.

Amazingly, so was the audience. They were laughing at Zade's antics and at the banter between them. When it came time for Lena to hand Zade the thimble, he monkey-crawled over to her, knuckles on the floor, and reached out his hand.

Lena went to hand him the thimble and—*bam!* Her fingers suddenly lit up.

She staggered back, yanking her hand away. Meanwhile, Zade's eyes widened in shock at the sight. Lena tried to hide her hands behind her back, but it was too late. He'd seen. And, she realized, so had the audience.

"Cool!" she heard a little kid in the audience say. "Her hands are glowing! How did they do that?"

If her hands were glowing, it meant Pearl was nearby. But where?

Suddenly—*crash!* The stage under Zade's feet gave way, and he vanished into a black hole. Lena gasped and staggered forward, realizing with relief that he hadn't simply disappeared. He'd fallen through the trapdoor in the stage. In the darkness below, she saw a hint of light. Pearl.

People in the audience gasped too. A few of them applauded, thinking it was part of the scene.

"Pearl! Stop it!" Lena hissed. "What are you doing?"

"He's doing it wrong," Pearl said. "He's supposed to take it seriously like Melissa said!"

In the faint light, she saw Zade stirring under the stage. He was all right. But, Lena realized, their scene wasn't. The audience was simply staring at her now, waiting for her to go on.

She scrambled to come up with her next line, but it was no use. Her mind was blank. And even if she did continue, she couldn't exactly do both parts on her own, could she?

Then she heard a voice from behind her. "Wendy?"

She turned to find her mom walking onto the stage. What on earth? What was her mom doing? Lena felt a wave of anger rush through her. Why couldn't her mom just leave her alone for once? Why couldn't she stop trying to fix everything?

But then Lena noticed something. Her mom's hands were shaking, and she was pale and sweaty, as if being onstage were torture. Lena realized that this was the first time her mom had been onstage in years. She wasn't doing this for herself. She was doing this to help Lena. And, Lena had to admit, she needed the help. Desperately.

"Wendy, I'm Tinker Bell," her mom said. "I was the light glowing in your hands."

Lena pulled herself together and asked, "You're the one who used your magic to make Peter disappear?" She forced out a laugh. "That was a neat trick. What do you want, Tinker Bell? What can I do to make you leave us alone?" But she wasn't talking to her mom anymore. She was talking to Pearl, who was now hovering in the middle of the stage.

"All I want is for Myrna's granddaughter to be safe," Pearl said. Her voice was so soft that Lena didn't think anyone in the audience could hear it. All they could see was a clump of light, "Tinker Bell," hanging above the stage.

"Look," Lena said, pointing to Miss Fine, who was sitting in the front row, looking a little horrified at how wrong everything was going. But she was also motioning for them to continue with the scene. "Look at all those people out there. They look happy, don't they?"

"Yes, we do!" a little boy called. And next to him, a little girl yelled, "I love you, Tinker Bell!" The other people in the audience laughed.

"But what if Myrna wants me to do something else?" Pearl asked. "She took such good care of me when I was sick. I promised her I'd take care of her too. And after she was gone, I promised to protect her daughter Martha and her granddaughter Melissa."

"You kept your promise," Lena said, still trying to make it sound as though she were talking to Tinker Bell. She only hoped Pearl would get the message. "You kept everyone safe, but now you don't need to protect them anymore. Peter might never grow up, but everyone else does. And that means you have to let them learn to take care of themselves."

"But I'm scared," Pearl said. "What if I leave here and I'm all alone again?"

"Don't be scared," Lena said. "We'll sing you a song." And

then she started to sing the tune Miss Fine had sung at the hospital, the sad, slow lullaby. Lena's voice shook, and she stumbled over some of the words, but then Miss Fine joined in to help her. At the next refrain, so did a few people in the audience. Soon, as more voices echoed through the theater, the song wasn't sad anymore. It was full of life and energy. It bounced off the walls and the ceiling, as if it wanted to be set free.

Lena reached out her hand, calling up her energy. But nothing happened. She narrowed her eyes and focused on getting her fingers to flare to life, but they remained unglowing.

Oh no. Could her new powers really be gone? What was she supposed to do now?

Suddenly, Lena felt her mom's hand in hers, and this time, she didn't pull away. Instead, she and her mom both held their free hands out to Pearl, urging her forward. Pearl came toward them and rested on Lena's fingertips, and then she let out a long, relieved sigh. Almost instantly, the ball of light sparkled like fireworks. The people in the audience gasped. And then there was a flash, and Pearl vanished.

After the show, Miss Fine came up and gave Lena a hug. "I don't know what happened up there. The lights…the song…

but it was beautiful. And I feel lighter somehow." She laughed. "I know that doesn't make any sense."

"It does," Lena said, realizing the haze around Miss Fine was gone. She wasn't haunted anymore. "Trust me."

"I can't believe I fell through the stage!" Zade said. "That was awesome!" He was limping around with a twisted ankle, but he didn't seem to care, not when everyone was going on about how amazing their scene had been and commenting on their amazing special effects.

Finally, when all the congratulations were over, Lena pulled her mom away from everyone. "Thank you," Lena said. "For rescuing me. For everything. You were right. I can't handle everything on my own. I thought I could, but…but if you hadn't helped me, I don't know what I would have done."

"You would have been fine," her mom said.

"Huh?"

Her mom laughed. "I realized after I'd rushed onto that stage that you didn't need my help."

"Um, yeah, I did," Lena said. "I mean, Zade fell into a hole! I was just standing on the stage, not doing anything. And then my hands started glowing!"

"But what you did next, that was all you. You sent that girl to the After. I had nothing to do with that. If I hadn't set foot up on that stage, you would have been fine. Just like you've been fine all these years on your own. It's time I accepted that."

Lena reached out and took her mom's hand in herself. "Maybe I didn't need you up there with me, but I'm glad you were. It felt like something we had to do together."

They stood there, hands joined, for a long moment. Any trace of the cold shoulder between them was gone. And even though Lena wasn't sure things between the two of them would ever be as easy as they'd been when she was little, she had a feeling they'd be a lot better from now on.

Finally, her mom gave Lena's fingers a squeeze and let go of her hand. "So your powers—my powers…?"

"I think they're really gone," Lena said. She should have felt relieved, but there was still a pit in her stomach. "Mom, I need to go home."

"Sure. Want to order some takeout when we get back to my place? It is New Year's Eve."

"No, I mean *my* home. And I need to get there tonight. By midnight."

Her mom blinked at her. "Tonight?"

"Please, Mom. Trust me. It's important. Really important."

She expected her mom to argue or to object. But instead, she only nodded and said, "All right then. Let's go to the airport."

⇉— Chapter 27 —➔

It was almost midnight and Marcus was armed with a spray bottle full of water, ready to squirt anyone who tried to lock lips as the clock struck twelve. Meanwhile, Natalie had sprinkled all the food on the snack table with garlic powder, and Connie had even made an announcement over the sound system saying that mono was going around and that people should *not*, under any circumstances, kiss at midnight. Most of the kids in the crowd had laughed, which didn't fill Marcus with a lot of confidence.

The fact that Lena wasn't here was making everything worse. Things had been so distant between them the past few days. Was that a sign of what was coming in the New Year?

As he glanced around the dance floor, he spotted Ann-Marie standing in the corner with both Peter and Albert. None of them looked very happy. Marcus hurried over, hoping a fight didn't break out. Though he couldn't imagine Albert fighting over anything except maybe how to properly tie a bow tie.

"What do you mean, you choose no one?" Peter was asking.

Ann-Marie's cheeks were flushed a deep red. "Look, I'm sorry. To both of you, okay? You're really nice guys, but I don't want a boyfriend right now. I don't want to even go out on dates. I don't have time."

"But we were having fun, weren't we?" Peter asked, clearly hurt.

"We were," she said. "But I think maybe we're better off as friends, don't you?"

Peter seemed to think this over for a minute. Finally, he nodded. "Yeah, I guess it was fun to have someone to talk about hockey with and stuff. But we can still do that."

"Totally," Ann-Marie said. "And Albert…"

He nodded slowly. "I knew it was too good to be true to have a girl interested in me."

"Of course there are girls interested in you!" Ann-Marie said. "Why wouldn't there be?"

"Well, because I'm—"

"You're great," Ann-Marie broke in. "Why do you think I keep trying so hard to beat you? If I can do better than you, then I know I've really accomplished something, right?"

Albert seemed to follow this twisted logic, because his face lit up. "Right," he said.

Then, amazingly, the three of them shook hands, and it was

over. After all of Marcus's work, all that scheming and worrying, it turned out Ann-Marie didn't want to be with anyone.

"Are you sure you really want to be alone?" Marcus asked her when she'd left the guys behind at the snack table.

She shrugged. "I thought having a guy around would make me happier, but honestly, I like being alone, always have. Why ruin a good thing?"

And the weird thing was, Marcus could actually kind of understand that. As a matchmaker, he spent a lot of time helping people not be lonely anymore. But he was starting to realize that being alone and being lonely weren't the same thing, not at all. And the aura around his sister proved it. It wasn't gray anymore. Even though she hadn't been matched with anyone, she was fine.

"I don't know how you do it," Ann-Marie added.

"Do what?"

"All this relationship stuff. It's exhausting. Being a supernatural matchmaker sounds impossible." She rolled her eyes. "I'm not saying I believe in any of that magic nonsense, but…" She shrugged and gave him something bordering on a smile. "You're a lot tougher than I thought you were."

Marcus could only stare at her in shock. His sister thought *he* was tough?

Suddenly, Marcus heard people around them chanting.

"Ten, nine, eight…" Marcus's shock turned to dread. "Three. Two. One. Happy New Year!" As everyone cheered, people started kissing all around him.

"No!" Marcus cried, running toward a couple and squirting them with water. They didn't seem to notice. He turned to Ann-Marie, who was also trying to break people up. "This isn't working!"

"The lights!" she cried. "Turn off the lights!"

Together, they ran through the hall, flipping off light switches. People only cheered, as if this were part of the merriment. Even when all the lights were off, people were still singing "Auld Lang Syne," and in the dim light, he could see couples smooching all around him.

It was pointless.

With a long sigh, Marcus started to flip the lights back on. He looked at Ann-Marie, who looked as defeated as he felt. Across the hall, Natalie was shaking her head as couples finally broke apart.

They'd failed.

Then he noticed something. Nearby, Albert was dancing with Connie. Except, when Marcus looked closer, he realized it wasn't Connie. It was a girl with similar hair and similar features, but she seemed shyer and less sure of herself as she and Albert had a hesitant conversation in between wild dance moves.

After a second, Marcus noticed the ugly horse scarf around her neck. The exact one he'd seen Connie wearing at the mall the other day. Then it clicked. This was Connie's cousin! Connie must have given her the ugly scarf as part of her make-over. This must have been the girl Albert had bumped into outside the comic book store. He was supposed to have been matched with her all along!

Marcus started to call up his energy, excited to zap them, before remembering that his powers were gone. But as he watched the couple dancing, their grayish auras swirling around them, suddenly, a spark ignited in between them, and then another, and another. As they danced and talked and laughed, their auras merged together, and soon, they weren't all gray anymore. They were lighter and brighter and quickly filling with sparks.

He couldn't believe it. The zap had worked without his powers! After all this time, his assignment was finally done! And to think, Connie had wanted to fix these two up all along. Maybe she really did know what she was doing.

At least that was one problem solved. Too bad everything else had turned out to be a total flop.

But as the crowd shifted, Marcus sucked in a breath. "Lena?" he whispered.

At first, he thought he was imagining things. Then she gave

him a big smile, and he saw it was really her. It was Lena. She looked exhausted and rumpled, but it was her.

"Marcus!" she said, rushing up to him. "I'm sorry it took me so long to get here! Am I too late? Is it past midnight?"

He didn't look at the clock. It didn't matter what time it was. Lena was here, and he wanted to kiss her. So he brushed her hair away from her face, and he leaned in, and he did.

As their lips met, the world around him began to spin. His ears started to ring, and he was suddenly so light-headed that he had to stagger backward, breaking the kiss.

"Whoa," Lena said, grabbing his arm. "I'm so dizzy."

"Me too," he said, clinging to her.

Then the ringing in his ears stopped, and as Marcus looked around, he realized the air around them was glowing. "Do you see that?" he whispered.

Lena nodded. "Do you think… Are our powers back?"

They rushed into the hallway to test out their powers, but when they called up their energy, something strange happened. Their fingers didn't flare to life with light, but there was something there. A faint glow, barely visible.

"They're back!" Marcus said. "At least sort of."

"But what does this mean?" Lena said. "Are they ever going to go back to normal?"

Suddenly, Natalie came rushing over to them. "Guys!" she

cried. "I had a vision! It was really faint, but I had one! We were working together with my dad—with Eddie—to fix all the things that have gone wrong the past few days. And some other people were there too. Connie and other kids with new powers, helping us."

"Connie?" Lena asked, clearly skeptical. "Connie Reynolds was helping us?"

"She'd actually make a pretty good matchmaker," Marcus couldn't help saying. "Once she learns how to follow the rules."

"So the power web's fixed?" Lena asked.

"Remember what Eddie told us?" Marcus said. "The web couldn't be patched up. It had to be rebuilt. Maybe we needed to reboot it."

"Why would the two of us being here together do that?" Lena asked. "And shouldn't we have kissed at midnight?"

But suddenly Marcus realized. "No. *Not* kissing at midnight, that's what broke the web. My sister's vision was about us!"

"But I wasn't even supposed to be here!" Lena said.

"The first time we kissed, it messed up the power web," Marcus said, things clicking into place in his brain. "And every time we tried to fix it, it just got worse because our powers were so interconnected. When you went to Arizona, the web snapped."

"But now we've started the New Year with a clean slate," Lena said slowly. "So that means…"

"Now that we're unconnected, we can do whatever we want and not worry anymore. Everything's finally fixed." Even though it didn't seem possible after everything they'd been through, Marcus felt sure it was true. Things were finally the way they were supposed to be.

Lena looked at him. "I wouldn't say we're unconnected," she said. "I...I'm sorry about the cold shoulder thing. All that scheduling phone calls stuff was stupid. And I didn't want us to be apart, Marcus. I just wanted us to be—"

"I know," he said. "But you were right. We're great when we're together, but that doesn't mean we can't have our own lives too."

For years, he'd let other people tell him what to do, trusting that Grandpa Joe or Eddie or Lena would help him figure things out. But for once, he'd had no choice but to take charge, and he had to admit that he'd actually kind of enjoyed it. Even if it hadn't gone the way he'd planned, for once, he hadn't just been on the sidelines. Maybe he could get used to that.

"Okay," Lena said. "Now that we *are* together and can do whatever we want without worrying about messing up everyone's powers again, I think the first thing we need to do is dance."

"Dance?" Marcus repeated.

"I have everything checked off my list," Lena said. "All the stuff I wanted to accomplish before I turn fourteen. Thanks to you, I did it all. First kiss. First date. All that's left is first dance."

"I don't really know how to dance," he said.

"I'll lead," Lena said. "It's not that hard."

But Marcus shook his head. "No," he said. "We'll take turns."

She laughed and took his hand. "I'm sure we can figure it out together."

Acknowledgments

Wrapping up a series requires lots of time and revision—and plenty of help. Huge thanks to Aubrey Poole for guiding me over the years and to Kate Prosswimmer for jumping in mid-series with reassuring enthusiasm. As always, many thanks to Ammi-Joan Paquette; to my writing group and critique partners; to the Writers' Loft and Simmons College communities; to my tirelessly enthusiastic family and friends; and to Ray, Lia, and Emma for the patience and the laughs.

About the Author

Anna Staniszewski was a Writer-in-Residence at the Boston Public Library and a winner of the PEN New England Discovery Award. She lives outside Boston with her family and teaches at Simmons College. When she's not writing, Anna reads as much as she can, takes the dog for long walks, and tries to keep her magical powers under wraps. Visit her at www.annastan.com.

THE DIRT DIARY SERIES

Anna Staniszewski

The Dirt Diary

EIGHTH GRADE NEVER SMELLED SO BAD.

Rachel Lee didn't think anything could be worse than her parents splitting up. She was wrong. Working for her mom's new house-cleaning business puts Rachel in the dirty bathrooms of the most popular kids in the eighth grade. Which does not help her already loser-ish reputation. But her new job has surprising perks: enough dirt on the in crowd to fill up her (until recently) boring diary. She never intended to reveal her secrets, but when the hottest guy in school pays her to spy on his girlfriend, Rachel decides to get her hands dirty.

The Prank List

To save her mom's cleaning business, Rachel's about to get her hands dirty—again.

Rachel Lee is having the best summer ever taking a baking class and flirting with her almost-sort-of-boyfriend Evan—until a rival cleaning business swoops into town, stealing her mom's clients. Rachel never thought she'd fight for the right to clean toilets, but she has to save her mom's business. Nothing can distract her from her mission...except maybe Whit, the cute new guy in cooking class. Then she discovers something about Whit that could change everything. After destroying her Dirt Diary, Rachel thought she was done with secrets, but to save her family's business, Rachel's going to have to get her hands dirty. Again.

The Gossip File

Some things are best kept secret...

Rachel Lee is visiting her dad at a resort in sunny Florida and is ready for two weeks of relaxing poolside, trips to Disney World—and NOT scrubbing toilets. Until her dad's new girlfriend, Ellie, begs Rachel to help out at her short-staffed café. That's when Rachel *kinda sorta* adopts a new identity to impress the cool, older girls who work there. Ava is everything Rachel wishes she could be. But when the girls ask "Ava" to help add juicy resort gossip to their file, Rachel's not sure what to do...especially when one of the entries is a secret about Ellie.

The Truth Game

Anna Staniszewski

THE TRUTH IS MORE THAN JUST A GAME.

Rachel Lee thought that ninth grade would be different. That she would be different. She'd get to hold hands with Evan in the hallway, become president of the cooking club...but it just feels like she and BFF Marisol are drifting apart. At first, Rachel thought the Truth Game app would be a great way to do a little anonymous confessing, to see how others handle their friendship fails. But when her painful truths become public, Rachel's in danger of losing her best friend—permanently.

THE MY VERY UNFAIRY TALE LIFE SERIES

Anna Staniszewski

My Very UnFairy Tale Life

THIS IS ONE DAMSEL THAT DOESN'T NEED RESCUING.

Jenny has spent the last two years as an adventurer helping magical kingdoms around the universe. But it's a thankless job, leaving her no time for school or friends. She'd almost rather take a math test than rescue a new magical creature! When Jenny is sent on yet another mission, she has a tough choice to make: quit and have her normal life back, or fulfill her promise and go into a battle she doesn't think she can win.

My Epic Fairy Tale Fail

FAIRY TALES DO COME TRUE. UNFORTUNATELY.

Jenny has finally accepted her life of magic and mayhem as savior of fairy tale kingdoms, but that doesn't mean the job's any easier. Her new mission is to travel to the Land of Tales to defeat an evil witch and complete three Impossible Tasks. Throw in some school friends, a bumbling knight, a rhyming troll, and a giant bird, and happily ever after starts looking far, far away. But with her parents' fate on the line, this is one happy ending Jenny is determined to deliver.

My Sort of Fairy Tale Ending

HAPPILY EVER AFTER? YEAH, RIGHT.

Jenny's search for her parents leads her to Fairyland, a rundown amusement park filled with creepily happy fairies and disgruntled leprechauns. Despite the fairies' kindness, she knows they are keeping her parents from her. If only they would stop being so happy all the time—it's starting to weird her out! With the help of a fairy-boy and some rebellious leprechauns, Jenny finds a way to rescue her parents, but at the expense of putting all magical worlds in danger. Now Jenny must decide how far she is willing to go to put her family back together.